Erika wasn't at all what he expected when he'd spotted a foreign princess on the guest list.

He'd envisioned either a stiff-necked dignitary or a football groupie bent on a photo op and a chance to meet his players. He didn't come across many people who dared tell him they didn't like football.

How contrary that her disinterest in his world made her all the more appealing. Yes, she aroused him in a way he couldn't recall having felt about any woman before.

And quite possibly some of that allure had to do with the fact that for once in his life he wasn't under the scrutiny of the American media.

Perhaps if he was careful he could do something impulsive without worrying about the consequences rippling through his family's world.

* * *

His Pregnant Princess Bride
is part of the Bayou Billionaires series—
Secrets and scandal are a Cajun family
legacy for the Reynaud brothers!

Dear Reader,

I'm thrilled to introduce you to a brand-new series! The Bayou Billionaires series launches this month with *His Pregnant Princess Bride*. Even more exciting, there will be a book out in the series every month for four months in a row! My best friend, Joanne Rock, and I are each writing two books in this Harlequin Desire series, taking turns alternating months. What a treat it is to work together on these stories set in the state of Louisiana, where Joanne and I first became friends and critique partners!

Bayou Billionaires features the four Reynaud brothers. With their ancestry rooted deeply in Acadian history, the Reynaud family first built their fortune in shipping, but hold a great love of football. All four sons inherited a passion for the game, playing in college and groomed for the NFL. While the eldest two sons broke ties with their father to bring corporate savvy to the front office of an emerging team, the younger two sons both continued their careers on the field. The Reynaud brothers are well-known in Louisiana, where their football exploits—whether in passing yards or in unconventional draft picks—are as much a topic of conversation as the women in their lives.

Be on the lookout next month for the next Bayou Billionaires story. As they say in Louisiana, *"Laissez les bons temps rouler!"* ("Let the good times roll!")

Cheers,

Catherine Mann

CatherineMann.com

HIS PREGNANT PRINCESS BRIDE

CATHERINE MANN

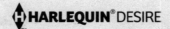

HARLEQUIN® DESIRE

ISBN-13: 978-0-373-73440-5

His Pregnant Princess Bride

Copyright © 2016 by Catherine Mann

Never Too Late
Copyright © 2006 by Harlequin Books S.A.
Brenda Jackson is acknowledged as the author of this work.

Recycling programs
for this product may
not exist in your area.

Printed in U.S.A.

www.Harlequin.com

CONTENTS

USA TODAY bestselling author **Catherine Mann** lives on a sunny Florida beach with her flyboy husband and their four children. With more than forty books in print in over twenty countries, she has also celebrated wins for both a RITA® Award and a Booksellers' Best Award. Catherine enjoys chatting with readers online—thanks to the wonders of the internet, which allows her to network with her laptop by the water! Contact Catherine through her website, catherinemann.com, find her on Facebook and Twitter (@CatherineMann1), or reach her by snail mail at PO Box 6065, Navarre, FL 32566.

Books by Catherine Mann

Harlequin Desire

A Christmas Baby Surprise
Sheltered by the Millionaire

Diamonds in the Rough

One Good Cowboy
Pursued by the Rich Rancher
Pregnant by the Cowboy CEO

The Alpha Brotherhood

An Inconvenient Affair
All or Nothing
Playing for Keeps
Yuletide Baby Surprise
For the Sake of Their Son

Bayou Billionaires

His Pregnant Princess Bride

Visit the Author Profile page at Harlequin.com, or catherinemann.com, for more titles!

HIS PREGNANT PRINCESS BRIDE
Catherine Mann

To my dear friend and former neighbor
from Louisiana—Karen.
Thank you for all the Mardi Gras cakes
and celebrations!

Prologue

"**I** have to confess, I don't care for the football at all."

Princess Erika's declaration caught Gervais Reynaud off guard, considering they'd spent the past four hours in the private viewing box overlooking Wembley Stadium, where his team would be playing a preseason exhibition game two months from now.

As the owner of the New Orleans Hurricanes NFL team, Gervais had more important things to do than indulge this high-maintenance Nordic princess he'd been seated beside during today's event, a high-stakes soccer match that was called "football" on this side of the globe. A game she didn't even respect regardless of which country played. Had it been sexist of him to think she might actually enjoy the game, since she was a royal, serving in her country's army? He'd expected a military member to be athletic. Not unreasonable, right? She was definitely toned under that gray, regimented uniform decorated with gold braid and commendations.

But she was also undoubtedly bored by the game.

And while Gervais didn't enjoy soccer as much as American football, he respected the hell out of it. The athletes were some of the best in the world. His main task for today had been to scout the stadium, to see what it would be like for the New Orleans Hurricanes when they played here in August. He'd staked his business reputation on the team he owned, a move his financial advisers had all adamantly opposed. There were risks, of course. But Gervais had never backed away from a challenge. It went against his nature. And now his career was tied to the success of the Hurricanes. The media spotlight had always been intense for him because of his family name. But after he'd purchased the franchise, the media became relentless.

Previewing the Wembley Stadium facilities at least offered him a welcome weekend of breathing room from scrutiny, since the UK fan base for American football was nominal. Here, he could simply enjoy a game without a camera panning to his face or reporters circling him afterward.

He only wished he could be watching the Hurricanes play today. He'd put one of his brothers in charge of the team as head coach. Another brother ran the team on the field in the quarterback position. Sportswriters back in the United States implied he'd made a colossal mistake.

Playing favorites? Clearly, they didn't know the Reynauds.

He wouldn't have chosen from his family unless they were the best for the job. Not when purchasing this team provided his chance to forge his own path as more than just part of the Reynaud extended-family empire of shipping moguls and football stars.

But to do that successfully, he had to play the political game with every bit as much strategy as the game on the field. As a team owner, he was the face of the Hurricanes. Which meant putting up with a temperamental princess who hadn't grasped that the "football team" he owned wasn't the one on the field. Not that she seemed to care much one way or the other.

Sprawled on the white leather sofa, Gervais tossed a pigskin from hand to hand, the ball a token gift from the public relations coordinator who'd welcomed him today and shown him to the private viewing box. The box was emptying now that the clock ran out after the London club beat another English team in the FA Cup Final. "You don't like the ball?"

She waved an elegant hand, smoothing over her pale blond hair sleeked back in a flawless twist. "No, not that. Perhaps my English is not as good as I would wish," she said with only the slightest hint of an accent. She'd been educated well, speaking with an intonation that was unquestionably sexy, even as she failed to notice the kind of football he held was different than the one they'd used on the field. "I do not care for the game. The football game."

"Interesting choice, then, for your country to send you as the royal representative to a finals match." Damn, she was too beautiful for her own good, wearing that neat-fitting uniform and filling it out in all the right places. Just looking at her brought to mind her heritage—her warrior princess ancestors out in battle side by side with badass Vikings—although this Nordic princess had clearly been suffering in regal silence for the past four hours. The way she'd dismissed her travel assistant had Gervais thinking he wouldn't even bother playing the diplomat with this ice princess.

"So, Princess Erika, were you sent here as punishment for some bad-girl imperial infraction?"

And if so, why wasn't she leaving now that the game had ended? What held her here, sipping champagne and talking to him after the box cleared? More important, what kept *him* here when he had a flight planned for tonight?

"First of all, I am not a reigning royal." Her icy blue eyes were as cool as her icy homeland as she set down her crystal champagne flute. "Our monarchy has been defunct for over forty-five years. And even if it was not, I am the youngest of five girls. And as for my second point, comments like yours only confirm my issue with attending a function like this where you assume I must be some kind of troublemaker if I don't enjoy this game. I must be flawed. No offense meant, but you and I simply have different interests."

"Then why are you here?" He wanted to know more than he should.

The PR coordinator for the stadium had introduced them only briefly and he found himself hungry to know more about this intriguing but reticent woman.

"My mother was not happy with my choice to join

the military, even though if I were a male that would not be in question. She is concerned I am not socializing enough and that I will end up unmarried, since clearly my worth is contingent upon having babies." Rolling her eyes, she crossed her long, slim legs at the ankles, her arms elegantly draped on the white leather chair. "Ridiculous, is it not, considering I am able to support myself? Besides, most of my older sisters are married and breeding like raccoons."

"Like rabbits."

She arched a thin blond eyebrow. "Excuse me?"

"The phrase is *breeding like rabbits*." Gervais couldn't quite smother a grin as the conversation took an interesting turn.

"Oh, well, that is strange." She frowned, tapping her upper lip with a short, neat fingernail. "Rabbits are cute and fuzzy. Raccoons are less appealing. I believe raccoons fit better," she said as if merely stating it could change a colloquialism on her say-so.

"You don't like kids?" he found himself asking, even though he could have stood and offered to walk her out and be done with any expectation of social nicety.

When was the last time he exchanged more than a few words with a woman outside of business? He could spend another minute talking to her.

"I do not believe I must have a dozen heirs to make a defunct monarchy stable."

Hmm, valid point and an unexpected answer. "So I take that to mean you're no threat to hitting on the players?"

Down on the field, the winning team was being mobbed.

"You assume correctly," she blurted so quickly and emphatically, she startled a laugh from him.

It was refreshing to find a woman who wasn't a sports groupie for a change.

He found himself staying behind to talk to her even though he had a flight to catch. "What do you do in the military?"

"I am a nurse by degree but the military uses my skills as a linguist. In essence, I'm a diplomatic translator."

"Say again?"

"Is that so shocking? Do I not appear intelligent?"

She appeared hot as hell, like a blue flame, the most searing of all.

"You're lovely and articulate. You speak English fluently as a second language. You're clearly intelligent."

"And you are a flatterer," she said dismissively. "I work as a translator, but now that I'm nearing the end of my time in military service, I'll be taking the RN degree a step further, becoming a nurse-practitioner, with a specialty in homeopathic treatments, using natural herbs and even scents, studying how they relate to moods and physiological effects. Stress relievers. Energy infusers. Or immune boosters. Or allergy relievers. Any number of combinations to combine an alluring perfume with a healthier lifestyle."

"Where do you study that?"

"I've been accepted into a program in London. I had hoped to pursue nursing in the military to increase my experience, but my government had other plans for me to be a translator."

A nurse, soon to become a nurse-practitioner? Now, *that* surprised him. "Very impressive."

"Thank you." She nodded regally, a lock of hair sliding free from her twist and caressing her cheek. She tucked it behind her ear. "Now, explain to me what I need to know to speak intelligently about what I saw down on the field with all those musclemen when I return home."

Standing, he extended an arm to her. "By all means, Princess, I know a little something about European football even though the team I own is an American football team."

She rose with the elegance of a woman who'd been trained in every manner to grace high-end ballrooms not ball games. And yet she chose to further her education and serve her country in uniform.

Princess-Captain Erika Mitras wasn't at all what he expected when he'd spotted a foreign dignitary on the guest list. He'd envisioned either a stiff-necked VIP or a football groupie bent on a photo op and a chance to meet the players. He didn't come across many people who dared tell him they didn't like football—European or American. In fact, he didn't have many people in his life who disliked sports. The shipping business might be the source of Reynaud wealth, but football had long been their passion.

How contrary that her disinterest in sports made her all the more appealing. Yes, she aroused him in a way he couldn't recall having felt about any woman before.

And quite possibly some of that allure had to do with the fact that for once in his life he wasn't under the scrutiny of the American media. Perhaps if he was careful, he could do something impulsive without worrying about the consequences rippling through his family's world.

He stepped closer, folding her hand into the crook of his arm, and caught a whiff of a cinnamon scent. "And while I do that, what do you say we enjoy London? Dinner, theater, your choice. Just the two of us."

Flights could be rescheduled.

She paused to peer up at him, her cool blue eyes roaming his face for a moment before the barest hint of a smile played over her lips. "Only if, after a brief outline of the differences in these football sports, we can agree to no football talk at all?"

"None," he vowed without hesitation.

"Then it sounds lovely."

Who knew cinnamon would be such a total turn-on?

One

Princess Erika Birgitta Inger Freya Mitras of Holsgrof knew how to make a royally memorable appearance.

Her mother had taught her well. And Erika needed all the confidence she could garner striding onto the practice field full of larger-than-life men in training. Most important, she needed all her confidence to face one particular man. The leader of this testosterone domain, the owner of the state-of-the-art training facility where he now presided. Players dotted the field in black-and-gold uniforms, their padded shoulders crashing against each other. Shouts, grunts and curses volleyed. Men who appeared to be trainers or coaches jogged alongside them, barking instructions or blowing whistles.

She'd finished her military stint a month ago, her hopes of serving her country in combat having been sidelined by her parents' interference. They'd shuffled her into some safe figurehead job that made her realize the family's Viking-warrior heritage would not be carried on through her. She'd been so disillusioned, adrift and on edge the day she attended the soccer game, she had been reckless.

Too reckless. And that weekend of indulgence brought her here. Now. To New Orleans. To Gervais.

Her Jimmy Choo heels sank into the most plush grass ever as she stepped onto the practice field of the New Orleans Hurricanes. She'd assumed this particularly American game was played on Astroturf. And assumptions were what she had to avoid when it came to her current adventure in the United States.

She had not intended to see Gervais Reynaud again after he left the United Kingdom. Their weekend of dates—and amazing, mind-blowing sex—had been an escape from rules and protocol and everything else that had kept her life rigidly in check for so long. She'd had relationships in the past, carefully chosen and approved. This was her first encounter of her own choosing.

And it had turned out to be far more memorable than she could have ever imagined.

She felt the weight of his eyes from across the open stretch of greenery. Or perhaps he had noticed her only because of the sudden silence. Players now stood still, their shouts dimming to a dull echo.

The rest of the place faded for her while she focused on Gervais Reynaud standing at the foot of the bleachers, as tall as any of the players. He was muscular, more so than the average man but more understated than the men in uniform nearby. She knew he had played in his youth and through college but had chosen a business route in the family's shipping enterprise until he had bought the New Orleans Hurricanes football team. The *American* football team. She understood the difference now. She also knew Gervais's purchase of the team had attracted a great deal of press coverage in business and sports media alike.

He had not told her much about his life, but before she made her trip here she had made a point of learning more about him and his family.

It certainly was amazing what a few internet searches could reveal.

Tracing their ancestry deep into Acadian history, the Reynaud family first built their fortune in shipping, a business that his grandfather patriarch Leon Reynaud had expanded into a thriving cruise ship company. Leon also turned a love of sports into another successful venture when he'd purchased shares in a Texas football team, learning the business from the inside out. His elder son, Christophe, inherited the shares but promptly sold them to buy a baseball team, creating a deep family rift.

Leon passed his intense love of football to his younger son, Theo, whose promising career as a quarterback in Atlanta was cut short due to injury and excess after his marriage to a celebrated supermodel fell apart. Theo had three sons from his marriage, Gervais, Henri and Jean-Pierre, and one from an earlier affair, Dempsey. All of the sons inherited a passion for the game, playing in college and groomed for the NFL.

While the elder two sons broke ties with their father to bring corporate savvy to the front office of the relatively new team, the younger two sons both continued their careers on the field. The Reynaud brothers were especially well-known in Louisiana, where their football exploits were discussed—as much a topic of conversation as the women in their lives. She'd overheard references to each in the lobby of the five-star hotel where she'd spent the night in New Orleans.

Would she be the topic of such conversation once her "encounter" with Gervais became public knowledge? There would be no way to hide it from his football world much longer.

Football. A game she still cared very little about, a fact he had teased her about during their weekend together, a weekend where they had spent more time undressed than clothed. Her gaze was drawn back to that well-honed body of his that had made such passionate love to her.

His dark eyes heated her with memories as he strode toward her. His long legs ate the ground in giant slices, his khakis and sports jacket declaring him in the middle of a workday. He stopped in front of her, his broad shoulders blocking the sun and casting his handsome face in shadows. But she didn't have to see to know his jaw would be peppered with the stubble that seemed to grow in seconds after he shaved. Her fingers—her body—remembered the texture of that rasp well.

Her breath caught somewhere in her chest.

He folded his arms over his chest, just under the Hurricanes logo stitched on the front of his jacket. "Welcome to the States, Erika. No one mentioned your intention to visit. I thought you didn't like sports."

"And yet, here I am." And in need of privacy out of the bright Louisiana sun and the even brighter curious eyes of his team and staff. She needed space and courage to tell him why she'd made this unexpected journey across the Atlantic to this muggy bayou state. "This is not an official royal visit."

"And you're not in uniform." His eyes glided over her wraparound dress.

"I'm out of the service now to begin furthering my studies." About to return to school to be a nurse-practitioner, the career field she'd hoped to pursue in the military, but they would not allow her such an in-the-field position, instead preferring to dress her up and trot her around as a figurehead translator. "I am here for a conference on homeopathic herbs and scents." A part of her passion in the nursing field, and a totally made-up excuse for being here today.

"The homeopathic scents for healing, right? Are you here to share specially scented deodorant with my players? Because they could certainly use it." His mouth tipped with a smile.

"Are you interested in such a line?" Still jet-lagged from the transatlantic flight, she was ill prepared to exchange pleasantries, much less ones filled with taunts at her career choice.

"Is that why you are here? For business before you start your new degree?"

She could not just banter with him. She simply could not. "Please, can we go somewhere private to talk?"

He searched her eyes for a long moment before gesturing over his shoulder. "I'm in the middle of a meeting with sponsors. How about supper?"

"I am not here for seduction," she stated bluntly.

"Okay." His eyebrows shot upward. "I thought I asked you to join me for gumbo not sex. But now that we're talking about sex—"

"We are not." She cut him short. "Finish your meeting if you must, but I need to speak with you as soon as possible. Privately. Unless you want your personal business and mine overheard by all of your team straining to listen."

She definitely was not ready for them to hear she was pregnant with the heir to the Reynaud family dynasty.

She was back. Princess Erika, the sexy seductress who'd filled his dreams since they'd parted ways nearly three months ago. And even though he should be paying attention to the deal with his sponsors, he could not tear his eyes away from her. From the swish of her curves and hips. And the long platinum-blond hair that made her look completely otherworldly.

He needed to focus, but damn. She was mesmerizing.

And apparently, every team member on the field was

also aware of that fact. From their top wide receiver Wildcard to running back Freight Train.

Gervais turned his attention back to finishing up his conversation with the director of player personnel—Beau Durant—responsible for draft picks, trades, acquiring the right players and negotiating contracts. An old college friend, Beau shared his friend's interest in running a football team. He took a businesslike, numbers approach to the job and wed that with his personal interest in football. Like Gervais, he had a position in his family's multinational corporation, but football was his obsession.

"Gervais, I'd love to stay and chat, but we have another meeting to get to. We'll be in touch," his former college roommate promised.

"Perfect, Beau. Thank you," he said, offering him a sincere handshake. Beau's eyes were on the princess even if he didn't ask the obvious question. Beau was an all-business kind of guy who never pried. He'd always said he didn't want others sticking their noses in his private life, either.

The eyes of the whole damn team remained on the princess, in fact. Which made Gervais steam with protectiveness.

He barked over to his half brother, the head coach, "Dempsey, don't your boys have something better to do than stand around drooling over a woman like pimply teenage boys?"

Dempsey smirked. "All right, men. Back to practice. You can stare at pretty girls on someone else's time. Now, move!" Henri Reynaud, the Hurricanes' quarterback and Gervais's brother, shot him a look of half amusement. But he slung his helmet back on and began to make his way into formation. The Bayou Bomber, a nickname Henri had earned during his college days at LSU, would not be so easily dissuaded from his obvious curiosity.

Dempsey scratched some numbers out on his paper. Absently, he asked, "What's with the royal visit?"

"We have some...unresolved issues from our time in England."

"Your time together?" Dempsey's wicked grin spread, and he clucked his tongue.

He might as well come clean in an understated way. The truth would be apparent soon enough. "We had a quiet...relationship."

"Very damn quiet if I didn't hear about it." Crossing his arms, he did his best to look hurt.

"You were busy with the team. As it should be."

"So you have some transcontinental dating relationship with Europe's most eligible princess?"

"Reading the tabloids again, Dempsey?"

"Gotta keep up with my players' antics somehow." He shrugged it off.

"Well, don't let her hear you discussing her eligibility. She's military. She might well be able to kick your ass."

"Military, huh? That's surprising."

"She said male royals serve. Why not females? She just finished up her time." Which had seemed to bother her. He understood well about trying to find where you fit in a high-profile family.

"Carole Montemarte, the Hurricanes' press relations coordinator, will have a blast spinning that for the media. Royalty for a girlfriend? Nice, dude. And she chased you clear across the ocean. You are quite the man."

Except that didn't make sense. She'd ignored his calls after he left the country. Granted, what they'd shared blew his mind, and he didn't have the time or energy for a transcontinental relationship. So his calls had been more...obligatory. Had she known that? Was that the reason she'd ignored him?

So why show up here now?

He sure as hell intended to find out.

Two

Limos were something of the norm for Erika. Part of the privilege of growing up royal. This should feel normal, watching the sunset while being chauffeured in the limo Gervais had sent to retrieve her from her hotel. Half of her childhood had been spent in the backseat of a limo as she and her family went from one event to another.

But today was anything but normal. As she pulled at the satin fabric of her dress, her mind began to race. She had never pictured herself with a brood of children like her sisters. Not that she didn't want them, but this was all happening so fast. And with a man she wasn't entirely sure of. Just the thought of Gervais sent her mind reeling. The thought of telling him about their shared interest made her stomach knot. She began to wonder about what she would tell him. How she would tell him. News she could barely wrap her brain around. But there were secrets impossible to keep in her world, so if she wanted to inform Gervais on her terms, she would have to do so soon.

Tonight.

And just like that, Erika realized the vehicle had stopped. Reality was starting to set in, and no amount of finery and luxury was going to change that. She had chosen the arctic-blue dress because it reminded her of her heritage. Of her family's Viking past. Of the strength of her small country. She needed these reminders if she was going to face him.

Try as she might, Erika couldn't get the way he looked at her out of her mind. His eyes drinking her in. The memory sent a pleasurable shiver along her skin.

The chauffeur opened the door with a click, and she stepped out of the limo. Tall and proud. A light breeze danced against her skin, threatening her sideswept updo. Fingers instinctively flew to the white-crusted sapphire pin that, at the nape of her neck, not only held her hair together but also had been in her family for centuries.

Smoothing her blond hair that cascaded over one of her shoulders, she took in the Reynaud family compound in the meeting of sunset with the moon, the stars just beginning to sparkle in the Louisiana sky. Though she had to admit, the flood of lights leading up to the door diminished the starlight.

She lifted her gaze to the massive structure ahead of her. Greek Revival with white arches and columns—no other word than *massive*, and a girl who grew up in a palace wasn't impressed easily.

As she walked up the stairs to the home, the sureness from touching her family heirloom began to wane. But before she could lose her nerve and turn back, the limo pulled away and the grand door opened in front of her. This was officially happening.

Though the lights outside had been clinical and bright, the foyer was illuminated by bulbs of yellow. The warmth of these lights reflected on what appeared to be hand-painted murals depicting a fox hunt. American royalty.

A servant gestured for her to walk through the room on the left. Gathering the skirt of her dress, Erika crossed the threshold, leaving behind the foyer and its elaborate staircase and murals.

This room was made for entertainment. She had been in plenty of grand dining halls, and this one felt familiar and impersonal, with wisps of silk that told their secrets to the glass and windows.

Erika had always hated dinners in rooms like this.

Quickly scanning the room, she noted the elaborately carved wooden chair and the huge arrangements of flowers and the tall marble vases. But Gervais wasn't here, either.

She pressed on through the next threshold and found herself in a simpler room. It was clear that this was a family room. The opulent colors of the grand dining room softened, giving way to a creamy palette. The kind of colors that made Erika want to curl up on the plush leather sofa with a good book and some strong tea with milk.

The family room sported an entertainment bar with

Palladian windows overlooking the pool and grounds. But if she turned ever so slightly she could also see an alcove that appeared to lead to a more private section.

The master bedroom and bath? She could envision that space having doors out to the pool, a hot tub, perhaps. She bit her lip and spun away.

It was not as if she was here to gawk at furniture. She had to tell a man she barely knew that they were having a baby. And that the press would have a field day if she and Gervais didn't get a handle on this now.

And there. She saw him. Chiseled. Dark hair, ruffled ever so slightly. His lips parted into a smile as he met her gaze.

Nerves and something else jolted her to life. Pushed her forward. Toward him and that wolfish smile.

She looked around and saw housekeeping staff, but no one else. Erika waved an elegant hand to the expansive room they stood in and the ones she'd already passed through. "Where's the rest of your family?"

"Dempsey owns the other home on the compound grounds, next door. My younger brothers Jean-Pierre and Henri share the rights to the house to the northwest on the lake. Gramps has quarters here with me, since this house has been in our family the longest. It's familiar. He has servants on call round the clock. He's getting older and more forgetful. But we're hoping to hold back time as long as we can for him."

"I am so sorry."

"They make great meds these days. He's still got lots of life and light left in him." A practiced smile pressed against his lips. It was apparent he was hopeful. And used to defending his grandfather's position.

"And where does the rest of your family live?"

"Are you worried they'll walk in on us?" He angled a brow upward, and she felt the heat of his eyes graze across her body. A flush crept along her face, heating her from the inside out. Threatening to set her nerves bounding out of control. She needed to stay calm.

"Perhaps."

"My father's in Texas and doesn't return often. Jean-Pierre is in New York with his team for the season and Henri lives in the Garden District most of the time, so their house here is vacant for a while."

Stepping out onto the patio, he nodded for her to follow. She hastened behind him. Intrigued. He had that way about him. A quality of danger that masked itself as safe. That quality that made him undeniably sexy.

And that, she reminded herself, was how she'd ended up in this situation.

Gervais surveyed the patio. She followed his gaze, noting the presence of a hot tub and an elaborate fountain that pumped water into the pool. The fountain, like the house, was descended from a Greek aesthetic. Apollo and Daphne were intertwined, water flowing from the statues into the pool.

Over the poolside sound system, the din of steel drums competed with the gentle echo of rolling waves on the lakeshore.

"You arranged dinner outside." Erika breathed in the air on this rare night of low humidity. She looked around at the elaborate patio table that was dressed for dinner with lights, fresh flowers, silver and china. Ceiling fans circled a delicious breeze from the slight overhang of the porch.

"I promised you gumbo—" he gestured broadly, before holding the seat out for her "—and I delivered."

She settled into the chair, intensely aware of his hands close to her shoulders. The heat of his chest close to her back. Blinking away the awareness, she focused on the table settings, surprised to realize he planned to serve her himself from the silver chafing dishes. "Your home is lovely."

"The old plantation homes have a lot of character." He slid into the seat across from hers. "I know our history here doesn't compete with the hundreds of years, castles and Viking lore of your country, but the place has stories in the walls all the same."

"The architecture and details are stunning. I can see why you were drawn to live here." When Americans talked about their colonial towns, they always spoke of the old-world charm they'd possessed. But that was selling it short. Cities like New Orleans were the distillation of cultures haphazardly pressed against each other. And that distillation yielded beauty that was so different from the actual Old World.

"If you would prefer a restaurant…" He paused, tongs grasping freshly baked bread.

"This is better. More private." She held up a hand. "Don't take that the wrong way."

"Understood. You made your point earlier."

Seafood gumbo, red beans and rice, thick black

coffee and powdery doughnuts—beignets. It was a spread that sent her taste buds jumping.

"Did you have a nice ride from the Four Winds Resort?"

"I did. The trees heavy with Spanish moss are beautiful. And the water laps at the roads as if the sea could wash over the land at any moment." The languid landscape was so different than her country's rugged and fierce Viking past. She'd liked learning about New Orleans so far.

"You could stay here, you know."

"I did not come here for that." She laced her words with ice even as her body burned with awareness of the man seated across from her.

"Then why are you here after walking out on me without a word or backward glance?"

So that hadn't escaped his notice. She began to prepare the speeches that had replayed in her mind since she had boarded the plane to make the transatlantic journey.

"I'm sorry about that. I thought I was making things easier for both of us. It was a fling with no future, given we live across an ocean from each other. I saved us both a messy goodbye."

At that time she had been thinking about the life she needed to get on track. But all her carefully laid plans were shifting beneath her feet, now that she was pregnant.

"And when I called you? Left messages asking to speak to you?"

"I thought you were being polite. Gentlemanly. And

do not get me wrong, I believe it honorable of you. But that is not enough to build a relationship."

"How much would it have hurt to return one call? If we're talking about polite, I expected as much from you." He cocked an eyebrow.

"You are angry. I apologize if I made the wrong decision."

"Well, you're here now. For your conference, right?"

"Actually, that wasn't the truth." She fidgeted with her leather band bracelet, inspirational inscriptions scrolled on metal insets providing support. Advice. And if ever she was in need of help, the moment was now. "I only said that in case others overheard. I'm here to see you. I want to apologize for walking out on you and have a conversation we should have had then."

"What conversation would that be?"

Oh, what a loaded question, she thought. "How we would handle it if there were unexpected consequences from our weekend together."

He stared at her, hard. "Unexpected consequences? How about you spell it out rather than have me play Fifty Questions."

She dabbed the corners of her mouth as if she could buy herself a few more seconds before her life changed forever. Folding the napkin carefully and placing it beside her plate, she met his dark brown eyes, her own gaze steady. Her hands shaky. "I am pregnant. The baby is yours."

Of all the things that Erika could have said, being pregnant was not what Gervais had been preparing himself for. He ought to say something. Something fast, witty and comforting. But instead, he just looked at her.

Really looked at her as he swallowed. Hard.

She was every bit as breathtaking as that first night they'd met. But there was something different in the way she carried her body that should have tipped him off.

Her face was difficult to read. She'd iced him out of gaining any insights in her eyes. Gervais examined the hair that trailed down her shoulder, exposing her collarbone and slender neck. This was the hairstyle of a royal, so different than the girl who had let her hair run wild over their weekend together.

And what a weekend it'd been. Months had passed since then and he still thought about her. About the way she'd tasted on his tongue.

He had to say something worthy of that. Of her. He collected his thoughts, determined to say the perfect thing.

Despite all of that, only one word fell out of his mouth.

"Pregnant." So much for a grand speech.

Her face flashed with a hint of disappointment. Of course, she had every right to expect more from him. But more silence escaped his lips, and the air was filled not with sounds of him speaking, but with the buzz of waves and boats.

The trace of frustration and disappointment had left her face. She looked every bit a Viking queen. Impassive. Strong. Icy. And still so damn sexy in her soft feminine clothes and that bold leather bracelet.

"Yes, and I am absolutely certain the child is yours."

"I didn't question you."

"I wanted to be clear. Although in these days of DNA tests, it is not a subject that one can lie about." She frowned. "Do you need time to think, for us to talk more later? You look pale."

Did he? Hell, he did feel as if he'd been broadsided by a three-hundred-pound linebacker, but back in his ballplaying days he'd been much faster at recovery. And the stakes here were far higher. He needed to tread carefully. "A child is always cause for celebration." He took her hand in his, as close as he could let himself get until he had answers, no matter how tempted he was for more. "I'm just surprised. We were careful."

"Not careful enough, apparently. You, um, did stretch the condom, and perhaps there was a leak."

He choked on a cough. "Um, uh…I don't know what to say to that."

"It was not a compliment, you Cro-Magnon." She shook her hand free from his. "Simply an observation."

"Fair enough. Okay, so you're pregnant with my baby. When do you want to head to the courthouse to get married?"

"Are you joking? I did not come to the United States expecting a proposal of marriage."

"Well, that is what I am offering. Would you prefer I do this in a more ceremonial way? Fine." He slid from his chair and dropped to one knee on the flagstone patio. "Marry me and let's bring up this child together."

Her eyes went wide with shock and she shot to her

feet. Looking around her as if to make sure no one overheard. "Get up. You look silly."

"Silly?"

For the first time since he'd met her, she appeared truly flustered. She edged farther away, sweeping back her loose hair with nervous hands. "Perhaps I chose the wrong word. You look…not like you. And this is not what I want."

"What do you want?"

"I am simply here to notify you about your child and discuss if you wish to be a part of the baby's life before I move forward with my life."

"Damn straight I want to bring up my child."

"Shared custody."

He reached to capture her restless hands and hold them firmly in his. "You are not hearing me. I want to raise my child."

"*Our* child."

"Of course." He caressed the insides of her wrists with his thumbs. "Let's declare peace so we can make our way through this conversation amicably."

Her shoulders relaxed and he guided her to a bench closer to the half wall at the end of the patio. They sat side by side, shoulder to shoulder.

She nodded. "I want peace, very much. That's why I came to you now, early on, rather than just calling or waiting longer."

"And I am glad you did." He slid his hand up her arm to her shoulder, cupping the warmth of her, aching for more. "My brother Dempsey grew up thinking our father didn't want him and it scarred him. I refuse to let that happen to my child. My baby will know he or she is wanted."

"Of course our child will be brought up knowing both parents love and want him or her."

"Yes, and you still haven't answered my question."

"What question?"

"The *silly* question that comes with a guy getting down on one knee. Will you marry me?"

Three

"Marry you? I do not even know you." Erika's voice hitched. Marriage? She had wanted him to be supportive, sure. But…marriage? The words tumbled over and over in her head in a disjointed echo.

"We knew each other well enough to have sex. Call me old-fashioned, but I'm trying to do the right thing here and offer to marry you. We can have a civil ceremony and divorce in a year. As far as our child knows, we gave it an honest try but things didn't work." His voice was level. Calm. Practical.

Her fears multiplied. This seemed too calculated. And she would not land in a family environment that was all for show again. Being raised royal had taught her she was not meant for a superficial existence. She had already chosen a meaningful career. A future where she could make a difference.

Swallowing back the anxiety swelling in her chest, she reminded herself to be reasonable.

"You figured all that out this fast? Or have you had practice with this sort of business before?" The notion cut her with surprising sharpness. She did not want to think about Gervais involved with other women after the way they'd been together.

"I am not joking." His hand inched toward hers.

She scrutinized his face, studied the way his jaw jutted. The play of muted lights on his dark hair, the way it was thickest on top of his head. Even now, he was damn attractive. But that fact wasn't enough to chase reason from her mind.

"Apparently not."

"I'll take that as a no to my proposal." Retreating his hand, he leaned forward, elbows on his knees.

"You most certainly can. It is far too soon to speak of marriage. And have you forgotten? I have plans to pursue my education in the UK."

Tilting his head, he lowered his voice. It became soft. Gentle. "You won't even consider my offer? Not even for the baby's sake? Let me take care of you while you're pregnant and recovering, postpartum and such. You can get to know my family during the football season. Afterward, we can spend more time with yours."

Even if the monarchy was defunct, she was a royal and sure of herself. She shot to her feet. "Do I get any say in this at all? You are a pushy man. I do not remember that about you."

He stood and stepped closer, very close, suggestively. His hips and thighs warm against hers. "What do you remember about our time together?"

"If you are trying to seduce me into doing whatever you want—" Erika needed to focus. Which was tougher than ever with him pressed up against her and that smolder in his eye setting her on fire.

"If? I must not be working hard enough." He slid his hands up her arms.

Her eyes fluttered shut, and for a moment she felt as if she could give in. But thoughts of her future child coursed through her mind. A ragged breath escaped her lips, and she reopened her eyes.

She clasped his wrists. "Stop. I am not playing games. I came here to inform you. Not demand anything of you. And certainly not to reenact our past together."

His hands dropped and he scowled. "Let me get this straight. If I hadn't wanted anything to do with the baby, you would have simply walked away?"

"You never would have heard from me again." The words escaped her as an icy dagger. She would have no use for such a man. And she had to admit that even if his proposal felt pushy, at least Gervais was not the sort of person to walk away from his child.

"Well, not a chance in hell is that happening this time. You may have brushed me off once before, but not again."

Had he genuinely wished to see her again after their weekend together? She had been afraid to find out at the time, afraid of answering his call only to discover that his contact was a perfunctory duty and social nicety. After what they had shared, she was not sure she could bear hearing that cool retreat in his voice. Now, of course, she would never know what his intentions had truly been toward her.

She took a deep breath. Regrouped.

"And you cannot command me to your will," she warned him, her shoulders stiff with tension. "I will not be forced into marriage because you think that is the best plan. I have plans, as well."

How many people had underestimated her resolve over the years because she had that label of "princess" attached to her? Her commanding officers. Teachers. Her own parents.

She would simply have to show Gervais her mettle.

"I understand that," he murmured, his voice melting into the sounds of waves and steel drums. "Now we need to make plans together."

Some of the tension in her eased. "Nice to know you can be reasonable and not just impulsive."

With a shrug, he began again. "In the interest of being reasonable, let's spend the next four weeks—"

"Two weeks," she corrected him. She had already disrupted her life and traveled halfway across the globe for him.

He nodded slowly. "Two weeks getting to know each other better as we make plans for our child. You could stay here in my home, where there are plenty of suites for privacy. I won't make a move that isn't mutual. We'll use this time to find common ground."

"And if we are not successful in your time frame?"

This felt like a business deal. But the time frame might be enough to bring him to reason.

"Then I guess I'll have to follow you home. Now, how about I call over to the hotel for them to send your things here? You look ready to fall asleep on your feet."

"You're honestly suggesting I give up my plans completely and stay here?" She gestured back toward the house. Two weeks. Together. Under the same roof.

That part sounded decidedly *less* like a business deal. The very idea wisped heatedly over her skin.

"Not in my bed—unless you ask, of course." He smiled devilishly. "But if we're going to make the most of these two weeks, it's best we stay here. There are fantastic graduate school programs in the area, too, if you opt for that later down the road. And I can also provide you with greater protection here."

"Protection?" What in the world did she need his protection for? And from what? And what was this later-down-the-road notion for her plans?

"We're a professional NFL family. That brings with it a level of fame and notoriety unrivaled in any other business domain. The fans are passionate. And while most of them are supportive, there is a segment that takes the game very personally. Some of the more unstable types occasionally seek revenge for what they perceive as bad decisions." His jaw flexed. "Since your child is my child, that puts our baby at risk as a Reynaud. If you won't stay here for yourself, then stay for our child. We are safe here."

He had found the one reason she couldn't debate. But she needed to be careful. To give herself time to think through the consequences of what she was agreeing to, and she couldn't do that now when she was so tired.

"I am weary. It has been a long, emotional day. I would appreciate being shown to these guest suites that you speak of and I will consider it."

"Of course." He picked up his phone and tapped the screen twice before setting it down. "You'll find all the toiletries you need at your disposal. I'll have someone show you to a room and make sure you have everything you need."

Before he finished speaking, a maid had arrived at the door, perhaps summoned by his phone.

Apparently, Gervais was serious about giving her some space if she elected to stay in the house with him. And while she appreciated that, she was also surprised at his easy efficiency. Hadn't her pregnancy announcement rattled this coolly controlled man even a little?

"Thank you." She looked at him, her breath catching at the raw masculinity of the man. She backed up a step, needing boundaries. And sleep.

"And I'll have a long Hurricanes jersey sent up for you to sleep in." His eyes remained on hers, but his voice stirred something inside her.

The last time they had slept under the same roof, there hadn't been much sleeping accomplished at all. And somehow, as she took her leave of him, she knew that he was remembering that fact as vividly as she did.

The door closed behind her, and she loosed a breath that she didn't realize she'd been holding.

This was...different from what she had grown up

with. The billowy sheer curtains thinly veiled a view of Lake Pontchartrain. Heels clacked against the opulent white marble as she made her way to an oversize plush bed. Instinctively, she ran her hand over the white comforter as she took in the room.

A grand, hand-carved mahogany-wood nightstand held a score of toiletries.

It was luxurious. She unscrewed the lid on one of the lotion bottles, and the light scent of jasmine wafted up to her. She set it down, picked up the shampoo, popped the lid and breathed in mint and a tropical, fruity flavor.

This house was old, not as old as her castle, of course, but it still had history. And such a different feel than her wintry homeland. This was grander, built more for leisure than practicality.

Plopping onto the bed, Erika was somewhat surprised to note the bed was every bit as comfortable as it looked. The bed seemed to wrap her in a hug.

And she needed a hug. Everything in her life was undergoing a drastic change. Untethered. That was where she was. Her career in the military was over. It left her feeling strange, adrift. The past few years, her path had been set. And now? A river of conflicting wants and obligations flooded her mind.

Yes, she wanted to pursue her dream. She wanted to be a nurse-practitioner and pursue her studies in the UK, wanted that so badly. But that dream wasn't as simple as it had been a couple months ago.

Even now, thousands of miles away, she felt the tendrils of familial pressure. When they learned she was going to have a child, they would be pressuring her.

Probably into marriage. And Gervais seemed to have the same ideas. How was she supposed to balance all of it?

In her soul, she knew she'd be able to take care of her child. Give her baby everything and have her dreams, too. But the weight of everyone's expectations left her feeling anxious. First things first, she needed to figure out what she wanted. How she would handle all of this. And then she could deal with the demands of her family and Gervais.

Lifting herself off the bed, she made her way to the coffee table where a stack of old sports programs casually dressed the table.

Dragging her fingers over the covers, she tried to get a feel for Gervais. For his family. The Greek Revival hinted at wealth but shed little on his personality. Though, from her brief time in the halls, she noticed how sparsely decorated the place was. On the wall, directly across from where she stood, were some photos in sleek black frames. They were matted and simple. The generic sorts of photographs that belonged more in a cold, impersonal office than a residence.

She walked over to investigate them further. The two images that hung on the wall were formal portraits, similar to the kinds she and her family had done. But whereas her family bustled with Viking grace and was filled with women, these pictures were filled with the Reynaud men.

The sons stood closer to the grandfather. Strange. A man who looked as if he could be Gervais's father was on the edge of the photograph, an impatient smile curling over his face.

Gingerly, she reached out to the frame, fingers finding cool glass. Gervais. Handsome as the devil. A smile was on her lips before she could stop it. She dropped her hand.

No, Erika. She had to remain focused. And figure out how to do what was best for her—their—child that didn't involve jumping into bed with him. Again.

Pulling at the hem of the jersey that cut her midthigh, a jersey she'd found on her bed and couldn't resist wearing, she resolved to keep her hands off him. And his out from under her jersey. Even if that did sound…delicious.

Father.

The word blasted in his mind like an air horn.

Gervais tried to bring his mind back to the present. To the meeting with Dempsey, who had stopped by after Erika retreated to a vacant suite for the night. Just because Erika was pregnant didn't mean his career was nonexistent. He needed to talk with his brother about the Hurricanes' development. About corporate sponsorships and expanding their team's prestige and net worth.

But that was a lot easier said than done with the latest developments in his personal life.

He swirled his local craft beer in his glass, watching the mini tornado foam in the center as he made himself comfortable in the den long after dinner had ended. Back when this house had still belonged to his parents, most of the rooms had been fussy and full of interior decorator additions—elaborate crystal light fixtures that hung so low he and his brothers broke a part of it every time they threw a ball in the house. Or three-dimensional art that spanned whole walls and would scrape the skin off an arm if they tackled each other into it.

The den had always been male terrain and it remained a place where Gervais felt most comfortable. The place where he most often met with his brothers. Dempsey had headed for this room as soon as he'd arrived tonight.

Now, sipping his beer, Gervais tried like hell to get his head focused back on work. The team.

Dempsey took an exaggerated sip from his glass and set it on the table in front of them. Cocking his head to the side, he settled deeper in the red leather club chair and asked, "What's the deal with the princess's arrival? She damn near caused Freight Train to trip over his feet like a first-day rookie."

"She came by to see me." Gervais tried to make it sound casual. Breezy.

"Because New Orleans happens to be right around the corner from Europe?"

"Your humor slays me." He tipped back his beer. Dempsey was a lot of things, but indirect? Never.

"Well, she obviously came to see you. And from what I'm starting to hear now from the gossip already churning, the two of you spent a great deal of time together in the UK. Are you two back together again? Dating?" A small smile, but his eyes were trained on Gervais. A Reynaud trait—dogged persistence.

"Not exactly dating."

"Then why is she here?" He leaned forward, picking up his glass. "And don't tell me it's none of my business, because she's distracting you."

He wanted to argue the point. But who the hell would he be kidding?

Instead, he dropped his voice. "This goes no further than the two of us for now."

"I'm offended you have to ask that."

"Right. Well, she's pregnant. It's mine."

"You're certain?" Dempsey set his glass on the marble side table, face darkening like a storm rolling out.

Gervais stared him down. Not in the mood for that runaround.

"All right. Your child. What next?"

"My child, my responsibility." He would be there for his child. That was nonnegotiable.

"Interesting choice of words. *Responsibility*." Something shifted in Dempsey's expression. But Gervais didn't have to wonder why. Dempsey was Gervais's illegitimate half brother. Dempsey hadn't even been in the picture until he turned thirteen years old, when Yvette, Dempsey's mom, had angled to extort money from their father, Theo, at which point Theo brought Dempsey to the family home.

To say the blending had been rough was generous. It was something that felt like the domestic equivalent of World War Three. Gervais's mother left. Then it was just a houseful of men—his brothers, Theo and Gramps. And it was really Gramps who had taken care of the boys. Theo was too busy shucking responsibilities.

"I'm sure as hell not walking away." He'd seen too

well the marks it left on Dempsey not knowing his father in the early years, the sting of growing up thinking his father didn't care. Hell, their father hadn't even known Dempsey existed.

Not that it excused their father, since he'd misled Dempsey's mother.

"I'm just saying that I understand what it feels like to be an inconvenient mistake. A responsibility." His jaw flexed, gaze fixed over Gervais's head.

"Dad loves you. We all do. You're part of our family."

"I know. But that wasn't always the case."

"We didn't know you then."

"He did. Or at least he knew that he'd been with women without considering the consequences." Dempsey's eyes darkened a shade, protectiveness for his mother obvious, even though the woman had been a negligible caregiver at best. "Anyhow, it took us all a long time to come back from that tough start. So make sure you get your head on straight before this baby's born. Better yet, get things right before you alienate the child's mother. Because if you intend to be in the kid's life, you're not going to want to spend years backtracking from screwing up with words like *responsibility* at the start."

The outburst was swift and damning. Dempsey shot up and out of his seat. He began to storm away, heading for the door.

Gervais followed.

"Dempsey—wait, I…" But the words fell silent as he nearly plowed into his brother's back.

Dempsey had halted in his tracks, his gaze on the

staircase in the corridor. Or, more accurate, his gaze on the woman now standing on the staircase.

Erika. In nothing but his jersey that barely reached midthigh. And she looked every bit as tantalizing as she had in her dress.

Gervais's eyes traced up, taking in her toned calves, the slope of her waist. The way her breasts pushed on the fabric. That wild hair of hers… She was well covered, but he couldn't help feeling the possessive need to wrap a blanket around her to shield her from his brother's gaze.

"I heard noise and realized there was someone wandering around." She drifted down a step, gesturing toward a shadowed corner of the hallway outside the den, where Gervais's grandfather stood. "I believe this is your grandfather?"

Gramps must have been wandering around again. Leon Reynaud was getting more restless with the years, and forgetful, too. But it was Erika who concerned him most right now. Her face was emotionless, yet there was a trace of unease in her voice. Had she overheard something in their conversation in the den?

Gramps Leon shook a gnarled finger at them. "Somebody's having a baby?" He shook his head. "Your father never could keep his pants zipped."

A wave of guilt crashed against him. For years he had tried to avoid any comparisons between himself and his father. Purposely setting himself on a very different path.

His father had been largely absent throughout his childhood and teen years. Theo Reynaud was a woman chaser. Neglectful of his duties to his children, his wife and the family's business.

Gervais would make damn sure he'd do better for his child. Even if Erika wasn't on board. Yet. He'd be an active presence in his future child's life. Everything his father failed to be.

Dempsey moved toward their grandfather, face slightly flushed. He stood and clapped Leon on the shoulder. "Dad's not expecting another child, *Grandpère*."

"Oh." Leon scratched his sparse hair that was standing up on end. "I get confused sometimes. I must have misunderstood."

Dempsey looked back at Gervais, expression mirroring the same relief Gervais felt. Crisis avoided.

His brother steered Gramps toward the door. "I'll walk with you to your room, Gramps." He gave Erika a nod as they passed her, though his focus remained on Leon. "I programmed some new music into your sound system. Some of those old Cajun tunes you like."

"Thank you, boy, thank you very much." They disappeared down the hall. Leaving Gervais alone with Erika.

Her arms crossed as she met his gaze. Unflinching bright blue eyes.

"You look much better in that jersey than anyone on the team ever did." God, she was crazy sexy.

"Whose jersey is this?" She traced the number with one finger, tempting him to do the same. "Whose number?"

He swallowed hard, a lump in his throat. "It's a retired number, one that had been reserved for me if I joined the team. I didn't." He shook off past regrets abruptly. He'd never played for the team, so he'd bought it, instead. "So shall I escort you back to you room?"

He couldn't keep the suggestive tone from his voice. Didn't want to.

She tipped her haughty-princess chin. "I think not. I can find my own way back."

That might be true enough. But they weren't done by a long shot. He wouldn't rest until the day came when he peeled that jersey from her beautiful body.

Four

She was really doing it. Spending two weeks with Gervais in his mansion on the shores of Lake Pontchartrain. She'd slept in his house and now that her luggage had been sent over from the hotel, she had more than a jersey to wear. She tugged at the hem, the fabric surprisingly soft to the touch, the number cool against the tips of her breasts.

This was actually happening. Last night had been more than just an overnight fluke. True to his word, Gervais hadn't been pushy about joining her here. But she felt his presence all the same.

And she was here to stay. A flutter of nerves traced down her spine as she fully opened the pocket doors to get a better look at the guest suite. She crossed the threshold from the bedroom to the sitting room, clothes in hand.

But she paused, toes sinking into the rich texture of the red Oriental rug. The way the light poured through the window in the sitting room drew her eye. Stepping toward the window, she took a moment to drink in the twinkled blue of Lake Pontchartrain.

The morning sun warmed her cheeks, sparking prisms across the room as it hit the Tiffany lamps. Glancing at her reflection in the gilded-gold mirror that was leaning on the mantel of the fireplace, she tucked a strand of hair behind her ear.

Mind wandering back, as it had a habit of doing lately, to Gervais. To the way his eyes lingered on her. And how that still ignited something in her...

But it was so much more complicated than that. She pushed the thought away, moving past the cream-colored chaise longue and opening the cherrywood armoire. As if settling her belongings in drawers gave her some semblance of normalcy. A girl could try, after all.

Her hand went to her stomach, to the barely perceptible curve of her stomach. A slight thickening to her waist. Her body was beginning to change. Her breasts were swollen and sensitive.

And her emotions were in a turmoil.

That unsettled her most of all. She was used to being seen as a focused academic, a military professional. Now she was adrift. Between jobs. Pregnant by a man she barely knew and with precious little time to settle her life before her family and the world knew of her pregnancy. She had a spot reserved for her in a graduate nursing program this fall, and she wanted to take coursework right up until her due date. But then what?

A knock on the door pulled her back to the present. She opened the paneled door and found a lovely, slender woman, wearing a pencil-thin skirt and silky blouse, tons of caramel-colored hair neatly pinned up. A large, pink-lipstick smile revealed brilliant white teeth.

She extended her hand. "Hello, I'm Adelaide Thibodeaux. Personal assistant to Dempsey Reynaud—the Hurricanes' coach. Gervais asked me to check in on you. I just wanted to make sure, do you have everything you need?"

Erika nodded. "Thank you. That is very kind of you to look in on me."

"I've been a friend of Dempsey's since childhood. I am happy to help the family." She wore sky-high pumps that would have turned Erika into a giantess—exactly the kind that she enjoyed wearing when she wasn't pregnant and less sure-footed.

"Did you have my things sent over?"

Adelaide's brow furrowed, concern touching the corners of her mouth. "Yes, did we miss anything?"

"Everything is perfect, thank you," she said, gesturing to the room behind her. "The home is lovely and comfortable, and I appreciate having my personal belongings sent over."

"We want you to enjoy your stay here in the States. It will be a wonderful publicity boon for the team to have royalty attending our games."

Erika winced. The last thing she wanted was more

attention from the media. Especially before she knew how she was going to handle the next few months.

Adelaide twisted her hands together, silver bracelets glinting in the sunlight. "Did I say something wrong?"

"Of course not. It is just that I am not a fan of football, or competitive sports of any kind." It was a half-truth. Certainly, no matter how she tried, she just didn't understand the attraction of football. But she couldn't tell Adelaide the real reason she didn't want to be a publicity ploy.

"And yet clearly you're quite fit. You must work out."

"I was in the military until recently, and I do enjoy running and yoga, but I have to confess, team sports have never held any appeal for me."

"No?" Adelaide frowned. "Then I am not sure I understand why you are here— Pardon me. I shouldn't have asked. It's not my business."

Erika searched for a simple answer. "Gervais and I enjoyed meeting each other in England." Understatement. "And since there is a conference in the area I plan to attend, I decided to visit." Okay, the conference was a lie, but one she could live with for now.

"Of course." Understanding lit her gaze, as if she was not surprised that Gervais would inspire a flight halfway across the world. "If you need anything, please don't hesitate to ask."

"Thank you. I appreciate your checking on me. But I am independent." She had always been independent, unafraid of challenges.

"I wasn't sure of the protocol for visiting royalty," Adelaide said, her voice curling into a question of sorts.

As if a princess couldn't fend for herself. "You are a princess."

"In name only, and even so, I am the fifth daughter."

"You're humble."

"I have been called many things, but not that. I am simply...practical."

Pink lips slipped back up into a smile. "Well, welcome to New Orleans. I look forward to getting to know you better."

"As do I." She had a feeling she was going to get to know everyone exceptionally well. Erika's thoughts drifted back to Gervais. She certainly wanted to get to know him better.

Adelaide started to leave, then turned back. "It might help you on game days if you think of football as a jousting field for men. You were in the military and come from a country famous for female warriors. Sure, I'm mixing time frames here with Vikings and medieval jousters, but still, if you see the game in the light of a joust or warrior competition, perhaps you may find yourself enjoying the event."

The door closed quietly behind her.

A joust? She'd never considered football and jousting. Maybe...maybe she'd give that a shot.

Her gaze floated back to the window, back to Lake Pontchartrain. It stretched before her like an exotic promise. Reminded her she was in a place that she didn't know. And it might be in her best interest to find any way into this world.

To make the most of these days here, to learn more

about the father of her child, she would need to experience his world.

And that meant grabbing a front-row seat.

Yet even as she plucked out a change of clothes, she couldn't help wondering... Had Adelaide Thibodeaux welcomed many other women into this home on Gervais's behalf?

Today was quite the production. Gervais watched the bustle of people filling the owners' suite at Zephyr Stadium for a preseason game day. Tickets for special viewing in the owners' box were sold at a premium price to raise money for a local charter school, so there were more guests than usual in the large luxury suite that normally accommodated family and friends.

His sister-in-law Fiona Harper-Reynaud was a renowned local philanthropist, and her quarterback husband was the golden boy of New Orleans, which added allure to her fund-raising invitation. Henri—beloved by fans as the Bayou Bomber—was the face of their franchise and worth every cent of his expensive contract. He was a playmaker with the drive and poise necessary to make it in the league's most closely dissected position.

The fact that female fans loved him was a bonus, even though it must be tough for Fiona sometimes. But she seemed to take it in stride, leveraging his popularity for worthy causes. Today her philanthropic guests sat casually on the dark leather chairs that lined the glass of the owners' suite. Half-eaten dishes with bottles of craft beer peppered the table in front of them as the clock ticked down the end of the second quarter that saw the Hurricanes up by three points.

Yet Gervais's eyes sought only one person. Erika.

He'd been busy greeting guests and overseeing some last-minute game-day business earlier, so he hadn't gotten to spend any time with her yet. She was tucked away, in a leather sofa by the bar, sipping a glass of sparkling water with lemon, wearing a silky, fitted turquoise dress that brushed her knees and caressed her curves with understated sex appeal. He knew full well where those enhanced curves came from.

From carrying his baby inside her.

She scrunched her toes in her heeled sandals, reaching down to press her thumb along the arch of her foot. The viewing box was cool—downright chilly. But was the New Orleans heat bothering her? The climate was a far cry from where she lived. He wanted to help her feel more comfortable, to love his home city as much as he did so they wouldn't be forced into some globe-hopping parenting situation. He wished they could have had a private breakfast to talk, but he'd been called away to the game. Thank goodness Adelaide had offered to check on her personally. Dempsey's assistant and long-time friend remained the one good thing that had come from Dempsey's early years spent living a hardscrabble life before their father had found him.

Adelaide had texted Gervais this morning, assuring him that Erika had everything she needed.

Now he watched Erika eyeing the food the servers carried. Caviar nachos and truffles pizza. Delicious delicacies, but she declined the offerings whenever the waitstaff stopped in front of her. Though she certainly looked hungry.

"Is the food not to your liking?" He stepped toward her, smoothing his tie and wondering if he should look into the foods native to her homeland. "We ordered a special menu for the event today, but we can have anything brought in."

Nearby, a group of women cheered as Henri connected with one of the rookie receivers running a slant route down on the field. No doubt, it would be one of Henri's last big plays of the game, since they needed to test the depth of the quarterback position with some of the backup talent.

Erika stood, moving closer to him, the scent of magnolia pulling his focus away from the game and slipping under his guard, making him recall their weekend together. Making him remember the view of her long legs bared just last night in a jersey that had covered her only to midthigh. He'd barely slept after that mouthwatering visual.

"Gervais, this is all incredible and definitely far more elaborate than I would have expected at a football game. Thank you."

Her response had been polite, but he could see something tugging at her. So he pressed, gently, "But…"

She took a few steps toward the glass, gesturing to the seats below, where fans were starting to crowd the aisles as halftime neared. "Honestly? My mouth is watering for one of those smothered hot dogs I see the vendors selling. With mustard and onions."

"You want a chili dog?" He couldn't hide a grin.

Right from the start she'd charmed him with the un-expected. She was a princess in the military. A sexy rebel. And despite all the imported fare weighing down the servers' trays, she wanted a chili dog.

"If it is not too much trouble, of course." She frowned. "I did not think to bring my wallet."

"It's no trouble." He wouldn't mind stepping out of the temperature-controlled suite into the excited crowd. How long had it been since he'd ventured out from behind the tinted-glass windows during a game? It had been too long.

He leaned to whisper in her ear, hand bracing her on the small of her back. "Pregnancy craving?"

She blinked quickly, her breath quickening under his touch. "I believe so. Mornings are difficult with nausea, but then I am starving for the rest of the day. Today has been difficult, with all the travel yesterday and jet lag."

"Then I will personally secure an order for you." He smiled. "I have to say I wouldn't mind having one for myself." He touched her shoulder lightly, aching to keep his hands on her. "I'll be right back."

Erika moved closer to the glass and took a seat, looking down into the field, her eyes alert.

There was no fanfare in yoga or running, so Erika looked on at the halftime show with a sense of wonder. LSU's band performed in tandem with a pop star local to the area, sending the fans into wild cheers as a laser light show sliced the air around her. The scents of fog and smoke wafted through the luxury suite's vents, teasing her oversensitive nose.

This box was quite different from the Wembley luxury suite where she'd met Gervais. The Reynaud private domain was decorated with family memorabilia, team awards and lots of video monitors for comfortable viewing in the back of the box right near the bar.

But she enjoyed her front-row seat, watching intently.

So this really did have a form of old-world pageantry mixed with a dash of medieval jousting. Her military training made her able to pick out various formations on the field below, the two teams forming and re-forming their lines to try to outwit one another. Viewing the game this way had been a revelation—and definitely not as boring as she'd once thought. And she couldn't wait to taste one of the chili dogs once Gervais returned.

Fiona Harper-Reynaud, the quarterback's wife and Gervais's sister-in-law, if Erika remembered correctly, tilted her head to the side. "Princess Erika, you look pensive."

"I have been thinking about the game, trying to understand more about what I've seen so far, since I am actually quite a neophyte about the rules. My sisters and I were not exposed much to team sports."

A few of the other women laughed softly into their cocktail napkins, eyeing Erika.

Fiona smiled, crossing her elegant legs at the ankles. "What an interesting choice, then, to spend time with Gervais when you're not a football enthusiast."

"I am learning to look at the game in a new light." She would read more about it now that she knew her child would be a part of this world.

She couldn't allow her son or daughter to be unprepared for their future, and that meant football. She could not sit in this box overflowing with Reynauds and fail to realize how deeply entrenched they were in this sport.

"How so?" Fiona traced a finger on her wineglass, her diamond wedding ring glinting in the light from a chrome pendant lamp.

Erika pointed down to the field, where the head coach and his team were now returning to the sidelines. "Adelaide Thibodeaux suggested I think of this as a ritual as old as time, like an ancient battle or a medieval jousting field. The imagery is working for me."

"Hmm." Fiona lifted one finely arched eyebrow. "That's quite a sexy image. And fitting. Armor versus shoulder pads. It works. I'll have to spin that for a future fund-raiser."

"That sounds intriguing." And it did. If it helped Erika to appreciate the game more, it could certainly appeal to someone else.

"Perhaps I should rethink the menu, too, as I may have overdone things with this event." She picked up a nacho and investigated it.

"The food is amazing. Quite a lovely, fun spread," Erika offered, smiling at her.

"But you want a chili dog—or so I overheard you say."

"I hope you did not take offense, as I certainly did not mean any." Erika fought the urge to panic. She bit down her nerves—and a wave of nausea. This was easily explainable. "I am in America. I simply want to experience American foods served at a regular football game."

A server walked by with another fragrant tray of caviar nachos—too fragrant. She pressed her hand to her stomach as another wave of indigestion struck, cramping her stomach.

Fiona's eyebrows rose but she stayed silent for a moment. "If you need anything, anything at all, please don't hesitate to ask."

Did Fiona know somehow, even though she didn't have children? There seemed to be an understanding— and a sadness in her eyes.

For a brief, fleeting moment, she wondered if Fiona had ever found herself in Erika's situation. Not the pregnant-with-a-handsome-stranger situation, but the other one. The one where she was an outsider who shouldered too much responsibility sometimes.

The weight of that thought bore down on her, making her stomach even more queasy. She fought back the urge, praying she could get to her feet and to the ladies' room before she embarrassed herself.

Erika bit her lip, shooting to her feet, only to find the ground swaying underneath her. Not a good sign at all, but if she could just grab the back of her seat for a moment to steady herself... There. The world righted in front of her and she eyed the door, determined. "I will be right back. I need to excuse myself."

And the second she took that first step, the ground rocked all the harder under her, and she slumped into unconsciousness.

Five

Gervais pushed through the crowds, eyes set on the chili dog vendor. As he weaved in and out, he saw recognition zip through their eyes.

The media had done a nice job planting his image in the minds of the fans even though he would have preferred a quieter role, leaving the fame to the players. But the family name also sold tickets and brought fans to their television screens, so he played along because he, too, loved the game and would do whatever was needed for the Hurricanes.

Many of the fans smiled at him, nudged a companion and pointed at Gervais. He felt a little as if he was in a dog-and-pony show. And while part of him wouldn't mind pausing to speak to a few fans and act as an ambassador for the team, he really just wanted to get Erika that chili dog. Pronto.

So he flashed a smile as he continued, stopping in front of the food vendor, the smell of nacho cheese and cayenne peppers sizzling under his nose. Of all the things Erika could have asked for, he was strangely intrigued by this request. It was the most un-princess-like food in the whole sports arena. He loved that.

Gervais's phone vibrated. He juggled the two chili dogs to one hand as he fished out his cell while taking the stadium steps two at a time. He glanced at the screen and saw his sister-in-law's name. Frowning, he thumbed the on button.

"Yes, Fiona?"

"Gervais—" Fiona's normally calm voice trembled "—Erika passed out. We can't get her to wake up. I don't know—"

"I'm on my way." Panic lanced his gut.

His hand clenched around the hot dogs until a little chili oozed down his fingers as he raced up the steps faster, sprinted around a corner, then through a private entrance to the hall leading to the owners' viewing box.

A circle of people stood around a black leather sofa, blocking his view. A cold knot settled in his stomach. He set the food on the buffet table and shouldered through the crowd.

"Erika? Erika," he barked, forgetting all about formalities. He dropped to his knees beside the sofa where she lay unconscious. Too pale. Too still.

He took her hand in his, glancing back over his

shoulder. "Has anyone called a doctor? Get the team doctor. Now."

Fiona nodded. "I called him right after I called you."

He brushed his hand over Erika's forehead, her steady pulse throbbing along her neck a reassuring sign. But still, she wasn't coming around. There were so many complications that could come with pregnancy. His family had learned that tragic reality too well from his sister-in-law's multiple miscarriages.

Which made him wince all the more when he needed to lean in and privately tell Fiona, "Call the doctor back and tell him to hurry—because Erika's pregnant."

Erika pushed through layers of fog to find a group of faces staring down at her. Some closer than others.

A man with a stethoscope pressing against her neckline while he took her pulse must be a doctor.

And of course she should have known that Gervais would be near. He sat on the arm of the sofa at her feet, watching her intently, his body a barrier between her and the others in the room staring at her with undisguised interest.

Curiosity.

Whispering.

Oh, God. Somehow, they knew about the baby and she hadn't even told her parents yet.

"Gervais, do you think we could have some privacy?"

He looked around, started, as if he hadn't even realized the others were still there. "Oh, right, I'll—"

Fiona stepped up. "I've got this. You focus on Erika."

She extended her arms, gesturing toward the door. "Let's move to the other side of the box and give the princess some air…"

Her voice faded as she ushered the other guests farther away, leaving behind a bubble of privacy.

She elbowed up, then pressed a hand to her woozy head. "Doctor, what's going on?"

The physician wearing a polo shirt with the team's logo on the pocket said, "Gervais here tells me you're pregnant. Would you like him to give us some privacy while we talk?"

She didn't even hesitate with her answer. "He can stay. He has a right to know what is going on with the baby."

The doctor nodded, his eyes steady and guarded. "How far along are you?"

"Two and a half months."

"And you've been to a doctor?"

"I have, back in my homeland."

"Well, your pulse appears normal, as do your other vital signs, but you stayed unconscious for a solid fifteen minutes. I would suggest you see a local physician."

Gervais shot to his feet. "I'll take her straightaway."

Erika sat up, the world steadier now. "But you will miss the rest of the game."

"Your health is more important. We'll take the private elevator down and slip out the back." He shifted his attention to the physician. "Doc, can you send up a wheelchair?"

She swung her feet to the ground. "I can walk. I am not an invalid. I simply passed out. It happens to pregnant women."

"Pregnant women who don't eat," Gervais groused, sliding an arm around her waist for support. "You should take care of yourself."

Even as she heard the grouchiness in his voice, she saw the concern in his eyes, the fear. She wanted to soothe the furrowed lines on his forehead but knew he wouldn't welcome the gesture, especially not right now.

So she opted to lighten the mood instead. Heaven knew she could use some levity after the stress she had been under. And how strange to realize that in spite of being terrified, she felt safer now with Gervais present.

She looked up at him and forced a shaky smile. "Don't forget my chili dog."

Gervais paced the emergency room. The hum of the lights above provided a rhythm to his pacing. He tried to focus on what he could control.

Which was absolutely nothing at this point. Instead of being in the know, he was completely in the dark. He couldn't start planning, something he liked to do.

Sitting still had never been his strong suit. Gervais wanted to be in the midst of the action, not hanging on the sidelines. That was how he'd been as a football player, how he dealt with his family. Always engaged. Always on.

But now? No one would tell him anything. He wasn't a family member. Not technically, even though that was his unborn child.

God, he hated feeling helpless. Most of all he hated feeling cut off from his family. His child.

What the hell was taking the doctor so long?

Sure, the place was packed with weekend traffic. To his left was a boy with what appeared to be a broken arm and a cracked tooth. His sister, a petite blonde thing, wrinkled her nose in disgust as he shoved his arm in her face.

The man on his right elevated a very swollen ankle. He was in the ER alone, sitting in silence, hands rough with calluses.

Gervais could hear snippets of the conversation going on in the far corner of the room. A young mom cooed over her baby, holding tight to her husband's hand. They were probably first-time parents. Nervous as hell. But they were tackling the problem together. As he wanted to with Erika, but the lack of information was killing him.

The whole ride over, Erika had been woozy and nauseated. He tried to tell himself that fainting wasn't a big deal. But he wasn't having much luck calming down his worries.

The possibilities of what could be wrong played over and over again in his head. He hated this feeling. Helplessness. It did not sit well with him.

A creak from the door called his attention back to the present moment. Snapping his focus back to the ER. And to the two men heading for him. His brothers Henri and Dempsey. Henri's sweat-stained face was grave as he caught Gervais's eye. Hell, he knew time had passed. But that much? And he hadn't even watched the rest of the game on the waiting room television.

He charged over to his brothers.

Henri hauled him in hard and fast for a hug, slapping him on the back. Smelled of Gatorade. Heavily.

The leftover jug must have been poured over his head, signifying victory. "What's the news?"

"I'm still waiting to hear from the docs." He guided both of his brothers over to the privacy of a corner by a fat fake topiary tree. "We won?"

Dempsey didn't haul him in for a brotherly hug, but he thumped him on the back. They were brothers. Not as close as Henri and Gervais, but the bond was there. Solid. "Yes, by three points. Even though we sidelined most of our starters to test depth at various positions. Henri's backup did a credible job marching the offense downfield for one more TD in the closing minutes. But that's not what matters right now. We're here for you. Is everything okay?"

Gervais shrugged. "We don't know yet. Nobody's talking to me. I'm not tied to her in any legal way."

Dempsey's voice lowered till it was something barely audible. He looked squarely into his brother's eyes. "Do you plan to be there for your child?"

"Yes." Gervais didn't hesitate. "Absolutely."

Henri shifted his weight from foot to foot. The three Reynaud men stared at each other, no one daring to utter so much as a syllable for a few moments.

Dempsey nodded. "Good. You know what? I'm going to get coffee for us. Who knows how long we will be here. ER visits are never short."

"Great. Thanks," Henri said as Dempsey walked back toward the doors. "Is she considering giving the baby up for adoption?"

"I didn't bring that up." Truth be told, he hadn't even

thought of that as a real option. It was his child. He wanted to provide for his child.

"Did she?" Henri crossed his arms, voice lowered so only they could hear each other.

"No. I'm not even sure how the royalty part plays into this." God, what if his power, prestige, money, wasn't worth jack and she took his child away altogether? "She discussed shared parenting."

Henri shrugged. An attempt at nonchalance that fell flat. "I just want you to know that if things change, Fiona and I are willing to raise the baby as our own."

Gervais looked over at his brother quickly, thinking of all the miscarriages his brother and sister-in-law had been through, the strain that had put on their marriage. This baby news had to be hitting his normally happy-go-lucky brother hard. "Thank you, my brother. That means a lot to me. But this is my child. Not some mistake. Not just a responsibility. My child."

Henri nodded and hooked an arm around his brother's shoulders. "I look forward to meeting my niece or nephew. Congratulations."

"Thank you." Gervais noticed how Henri's face became blank. Distant. "Are you and Fiona okay?"

"Sure, we're fine," Henri replied a bit too quickly.

"We need your total commitment to the season. If you're having any problems, you can come to me." And he meant it. He wanted to be there for his brother. For his whole family. They meant everything to him.

Henri shook his head, looking his brother in the eyes. Offering a smile that refused to light his cheeks or touch his eyes. "No problem."

Gervais shook his head, raising an eyebrow at him. "You never were a good liar."

Wasn't that the truth? When they were kids, Henri always cracked under pressure. His eyes would widen when he fibbed.

"No problems that will distract me from the game. Now stop being the owner of the team and let's be brothers."

Gervais was about to protest, but suddenly the ER waiting room was alive with movement. Dempsey strode back over to them, cups of coffee on a tray. A damn fine balancing act going on.

And following closely on his heels was a doctor. The same old, frazzle-haired doctor that had been treating Erika. His gut knotted.

The doctor cleared his throat. "Mr. Reynaud—Gervais Reynaud," he clarified. The whole town knew the Reynauds, so no doubt the doctor recognized them. "Ms. Mitras is asking for you."

All he could do was nod. Deep in his chest, his heart thudded. Afraid. He was afraid of what was wrong with Erika and his child.

The doctor opened a thick pinewood door to a small exam room and gestured for Gervais to enter.

In the center of the room, Erika was hooked up to a smattering of machines. Lights flashed from various pieces of equipment. Her blond hair was tied back into a topknot, exposing the angles of her face. Somehow making her seem impossibly beautiful despite the presence of the machines.

Within moments he was at her side. He wanted to

show her he was here. He was committed to their child and would not abandon her. Stroking her hand, he knelt beside her. "You're okay? The baby's okay?"

Her face was pale, but she smiled, her eyes serene. "We are fine. Absolutely fine."

"This child is important to me. You are important to me." She was damn important. He had to make her see that.

"Because I am the baby's mother." The words spilled from her mouth matter-of-factly. As if there was no other reason he'd be here right now.

"We had a connection before that."

A dramatic sigh loosed from her pink lips. "We had an affair."

"I called you afterward." She'd been imprinted on his brain. A woman he could not—would not—forget.

"You are a gentleman. I appreciate that. In fact, that was part of what drew me to do something so uncharacteristic. But it was only a weekend."

"A weekend with lasting consequences." A weekend that had turned him inside out. Given time, he could make her see that, too.

"More than we realized," she said with a shaky laugh.

"What do you mean?" Head cocking to the side, he tried to discern the cause of the uneasy laughter.

She gestured to the ultrasound machine next to her. "I am pregnant with twins."

Gervais tore his gaze from Erika, focusing on the screen. Sure enough, there were two little beans on the ultrasound. He and Erika were going to have twins.

Six

Exhausted, Erika relaxed back into the passenger seat of Gervais's luxury SUV. The leather seat had the smell of a woodsy cologne, a smell she distinctively recognized as Gervais. It was oddly comforting, a steadying moment in a day that had been anything but stable.

As the car pulled away from the hospital, she glanced out the window, craning to see the collection of Reynaud brothers who stood at the entrance. Her sisters would swoon over the attractive picture they presented, those powerful, broad-shouldered men. They had all come rushing to the hospital, filled with concerns. And likely, with questions.

But they had been polite in the lobby after her release. They didn't press for information—the conversation had been brief. They'd wanted to know if she was okay. And neither Gervais nor Erika had offered any information about twins. That was something that they still had to discuss together. Something she still hadn't processed.

But how should she broach this new development in an already emotionally charged day? How in the world could she bring up everything in her whirring mind? Her eyes remained fixed out of the car, even though the scene of the hospital had faded from vision, framed by wrought-iron fences and thick greenery. Now the vibrant pinks and yellows of the old French houses populated her view.

Glancing at an elaborate wood-carved balcony, she let out an emotional sigh. What had happened today had left her shaken. She'd never passed out like that before, never felt so disoriented in her life. She'd been blessed with good health, and she had pushed her physical endurance to the limit during her military training. Yet this pregnancy was only just beginning and it had already landed her flat on her back. But, thanks to Gervais's quick action, she and her children—*children*, plural, oh, God—were safe.

It was all that mattered. That her children were okay. The twins were fine. *Twins*. She turned the word over. Was it possible to love them both so much already, even though she'd just learned about them? And yet, she did. In spite of her nerves, in spite of not having a plan figured out. Sure, she was scared about the future, about having to deal with her family…but she was overwhelmed with a deep love for her children already.

She peered over at the man in the driver's seat beside her. Perhaps he felt her eyes on him, because soon Gervais's throat moved in a long swallow. "Twins?" he mused aloud. "Twins."

The simple utterance seemed to linger on his tongue and echo through the quiet interior of the luxury vehicle. Not that she could blame him for being overwhelmed by the news. There was a lot to take in. Still, even under Gervais's audible processing of the fact that he was about to be a father not to one but two children, she could hear a glow of pride in his tone. A protectiveness that caught her attention.

Of course, the raw, masculine appeal of his muscular body taking up too much space beside her might have something to do with how thoroughly he held her notice. How easy it would be to simply lean closer. Lean on him. She could almost imagine the feel of his suit jacket beneath her cheek if she laid her head on his shoulder and curled up against his chest.

She forced herself to focus on the conversation they needed to have instead. On their children.

"Yes, there are two in there. I even heard the heartbeats." Her heart fluttered with joy as she remembered the delicate beating of her—*their*—children. The sound had made her spring to life in a way she didn't know was possible. She felt bad he'd missed that. They were his children, too, and he'd deserved to have that same feeling of awe. Looking at him sidelong, she said cautiously, "Next time you can come with me if you wish."

"I wish." There was no mistaking the sound of his commitment.

"Then you should be there." She couldn't hold back

the smile swelling inside her as she drank in his eyes alight with honest excitement. "It is too early to distinguish the sex, you know."

He shrugged, clearly unconcerned. "That doesn't matter."

"It did in my family." It came out in a whisper, something almost like a secret. And each word hurt.

He glanced over at her briefly before turning his eyes back to the road as they drove west toward his home. "Be clearer for me."

She smoothed the skirt of her dress, wrinkled beyond recognition after being crumpled into a hospital bag during her exam. If only she could smooth over her past as easily. This was knowledge she carried every day. Knowledge that ate at her and had her entire lifetime. "A line of girls was always cause for concern in my home. The monarchy is technically inactive, but even so there is no provision for a female ruler. There are no male heirs. I am afraid…"

"Oh, no. No way in hell is anyone taking my children away." His brow furrowed, anger simmering in his eyes, the joyous warmth gone.

"Our children. These are our children." She felt all the same protective instincts he did, and she felt them with a mother's fierce love.

"And we can't afford to forget for even a moment how important it is that we work together for the children. If there's a chance we can have more than a bicoastal parenting relationship, don't you think it's worth figuring that out as soon as possible?" The look he gave her was pointed. Sharp.

But Erika wasn't about to back down. She hadn't decided how to handle whatever was between them. And that meant she had to think a bit more. She wouldn't be rash and impulsive. One of them had to think through their actions.

"I will let you know when I schedule my doctor visit. I will want to visit the doctor again before returning home."

He scowled. "Can we not talk about you leaving? We're still settling details."

"You know I do not live here." New Orleans was lovely, with its vibrant history, loud colors and live music that seemed to drift up from every street corner. But it was not home. Not that she really knew where home was these days...

"One day at a time. And today we are dealing with a big change, the reality of two children. I know that happens. I just never expected..." His voice trailed, his words ebbing with emotion.

"I have twin sisters." She had always envied them their closeness, like having a built-in best friend from birth. "Twins—how do you say?—walk in my family."

"Run in your family. Okay."

She blinked at him, filing away the turn of English phrasing that brought a funny image to her mind of twins sprinting through her family tree. This was all happening so fast, she'd never stopped to consider the possibility of twins. There was so much to figure out still. "My oldest sister also has twin girls. I should have considered this possibility but I have been so overwhelmed since I realized I was expecting."

"Thank you for coming to tell me so soon." He covered her hand on the center console. "I appreciate that you didn't delay."

"You are the father. You deserve to know that." Erika lifted her chin up, tilting her head to the side to get a better look at him. He was a good man. She knew that much.

"We're going to make this work." He lifted her hand and kissed the back, then the inside of her wrist over her rapidly beating pulse.

The press of his mouth to her skin was warm and arousing, stirring memories of their weekend together. The air crackled between them now as it had then. Her emotions were already in turmoil after the scare at the game. She ached to move closer, to feel his arms around her. To have those lips on her body again. Everywhere. Arousing her to such heights her head spun at the thought. How quickly she could simply lose herself in what he could make her feel.

But doing so would take away any chance of objectivity. And now she had twice the reason to tread carefully into the future.

The silver stain of moonlight washed over the lake. The water was restless. Frothy. Uneasy. A lot like the restlessness inside Gervais. But he had to pull it together in order to make this phone call.

He thumbed through his phone, finding his father in his contact list. How long had it been since they'd spoken? Months, no doubt. The bright screen blared at him.

He knew he had to call him about Erika's pregnancy.

Theo was in Paris for the week with his latest girlfriend. Which was, in some ways, fortunate. This way, Gervais had gotten to talk to Erika privately before his father had a chance at royally screwing the dynamic up.

But it also meant he had to make this call. Which was something he never looked forward to doing. Years of neglect and dysfunction had their way of clinging to their current relationship. Another lesson of how not to treat children brought to you by Theo Reynaud. Dear old dad loved football and his family, but not as much as romancing women.

Before he could think better of it, Gervais pressed Send on the screen. Feeling the pinch of nerves, he poured himself a glass of bourbon from the pool-deck bar, staring at where a few kids messed around with a stand-up paddleboard. Beyond them, the lights of gambling boats winked in the distance and even farther behind those he could see the bridge that spanned the lake.

Gervais wasn't sure why he felt the need to talk to his dad other than doing him the courtesy of making sure he didn't hear via the grapevine. Discretion wasn't Theo's strong suit. But if Gervais spun the news just right, maybe he could keep a lid on it a bit longer. Erika would appreciate that.

And tonight making Erika relaxed and happy felt like the first priority on a quickly shifting list in his life. But knowing that she carried his children had brought things into sharp focus for him today.

"Hello, son." His father's graveled voice shot through the receiver, yanking him from his thoughts.

Might as well cut to the chase.

"Dad, you're going to be a grandfather."

"About damn time. Damn shame Henri is still carrying a grudge and didn't tell me himself. The divorce was a long time ago."

In the background of the call, the sound of violin music and muted chatter combined with the clink of glasses. The sounds of a bar scene.

Gervais ignored the mention of his parents' dysfunctional marriage. "Henri and Fiona aren't expecting. I'm the one about to make you a gramps."

News about the twins could wait. One step at a time. He was still reeling from that news himself.

"With who? You didn't knock up some groupie looking for a big payoff from the family?" His voice crackled through the phone from across the Atlantic.

"Dad, that's your gig. Not mine." And just like that, he was on the defensive. Gervais was not his father. He would never be like his father. And the fact that his father thought he had that in his nature sent him reeling.

"No need to be disrespectful." Bells chimed in the background of the call, an unmistakable sound of a slot machine in payoff mode.

So much for keeping the subject of his parents' divorce off the table. "You destroyed your marriage with your affairs. You ignored your own sons for years. I lost respect for you a long time ago."

"Then why are you here now telling me about this baby?"

Gervais closed his eyes, blotting out the lights from the distant boats on the lake, listening to the sound of the water. With his spare hand, he pressed on his eyes, inhaling deeply. Exhaling hard, he opened his eyes, resolve renewed.

"Because this news is going to go viral soon and I want to make sure you understand I will not tolerate any inappropriate or hurtful comments to the mother of my child." That was something he absolutely would not allow. From anyone. Least of all his father. He would protect Erika from that.

"Understood. And who might this woman be?" An air of interest infused his words.

"Erika Mitras." He sat down, inspecting his ice cubes as he waited for his father to make some sort of off-color remark.

"Mitras? From that royal family full of girls? Well, hell, son. It's tough to find someone not out for our money, but kudos to you. You found a woman who doesn't need a damn thing from you."

The words cut him, even though, for once, his father hadn't meant any harm by them. Erika had said as much about not needing Gervais's help. But he wanted to be there for his children. For her. Seeing those two tiny lives on that monitor today had blown him away.

And knowing that Erika was already taxed from travel and devoting her beautiful body to nurture those children made him want to slay dragons for her. Or, at the very least, put a roof over her head and see to her every need.

"Thanks. That wasn't forefront in my mind at the time."

"When you were in England, I assume?"

"Not your business."

"You always were a mouthy bastard." Smug words from the other end of the receiver.

"Just like my old man." He downed half of his glass of bourbon. "Be nice."

"The team's winning. That always puts me in a good mood."

"Nice to know you care." Not that his father owned a cent of this team. The Hurricanes belonged to Gervais and Gervais alone.

"Congratulations, Papa. Name the little one after me and I'll give—"

"Dad, stop. No need to try so hard to be an ass."

"I'm not trying. Good night, son. Congrats."

The line went dead. So much for father-son bonding time.

Gervais tossed his cell phone on a lounge chair and tipped back the rest of the ten-year-old bourbon, savoring the honey-and-spice finish in an effort to dispel the sour feel left by the phone call. He didn't know what he'd expected from his old man. That he would magically change into…what? A real father? Some kind of reassurance that maybe, just maybe, he himself could be a good father to not just one but two babies?

Foolishness, that. Theo remained as selfish as they came.

Regardless, though, he knew one thing for certain. He was not going to ditch his responsibility the way his father had.

Tucked in the big guest bed in Gervais's house, Erika snuggled deeper beneath the lightweight comforter, hugging the pillow closer as sleep tugged her further under. She was exhausted after the hospital visit and the strain of pregnancy that seemed to drain all her physical resources. She would feel better after she rested, and she couldn't deny taking extra pleasure at sleeping under the same roof as Gervais.

During her waking hours, she did all in her power to keep the strong attraction at bay so she could make smart decisions about her future. Her children's future. But just now, with sleep pulling her under, and her body so perfectly comfortable, she couldn't resist the lure of thinking about Gervais. His touch. His taste...

Her memories and dreams mingling, filling her mind and drugging her senses with seductive images...

The press of Gervais's lips on hers sparked awareness deep in Erika's stomach. He pulled back from the passionate kiss, and she surprised herself when she was disappointed. She wanted his lips on hers. And not just there. Everywhere.

But he led her toward the couch in his den.

His den?

A part of her brain realized this was not a memory. She was in Gervais's house. In Louisiana. She could smell the scent of the lake mingling with the woodsy spice of his aftershave as he drew her down to the leather couch, tossing aside a football before he landed on the cushion while she melted into his lap. And it felt right. Natural. As if she belonged here with him.

Her heart slugged hard in her chest, the strength and warmth of his so incredible she could stay for hours. Longer. She wanted this. Wanted him. She'd never felt

*so alive as during those days when she'd been in his
bed, and she couldn't wait to feel that spark inside her
again. The hitch in her breath. The pleasure of sharp
orgasms undulating through her body, again and again.*

*Now he tilted her chin up, searched her eyes for
something. A mingle of nerves, anticipation and desire
thumped in her chest as he kissed her forehead. Her
lips. Her neck. She trembled as he touched her, her
whole body poised for the fulfillment he could provide.*

*Her eyes closed, and the muted noise of a football
game on a television behind them began to fade away
until only the sound of their mingled breaths remained.*

*"Erika," he whispered in her ear before kissing her
neck again. The heat of his breath on her skin made
her toes curl.*

"Mmm?" A half question stuck on her lips.

*"Stay here with me." His request was spoken in clips
between kisses, then a nip on her earlobe.*

*His hands tugged at the heavy jeweled collar around
her neck. He removed it from her, the metal crown
charms clanking against the coffee table. How good it
felt to set that weight aside.*

*"Let me take care of you. Of them." Wandering
hands found her shoulders, slipped underneath the
thin straps of her dress. She burst to life, pressing into
him with a new urgency. A want and need so unfamil-
iar to her.*

*As he kissed her, he rocked her back and forth. The
scent of earthy cologne seemed to grow stronger. De-
manded more of her attention...*

"Erika?" a deep voice called, a man's voice.

Gervais.

Opening her eyes, she had a moment of panic. This was not the hotel room.

As the suite came into focus, she realized where—and when—she was. This was Gervais's house, his guest bedroom. She wasn't in London, but rather in Louisiana. Still, the memory pounded at her mind and through her veins.

She wanted to go back there now. To her dreamworld in all its brilliant simplicity.

But Gervais himself stood in the doorway of the guest suite.

His square jaw flexed, the muscles in his body tensed, backlit from a glowing sconce in the hall.

"Erika?" He crossed the threshold, deeper into the room, his gaze intense as he studied her. "I heard you cry out. I was worried. Are you okay? The babies?"

The mattress dipped as he sat beside her, stirring heated memories of her dream.

"I am fine. I was, um, just restless." The sensuality of her dream still filled her, making her all the more aware of his hip grazing hers through the lightweight blanket. The electricity between them was not waning. If anything, she felt the space between them grow even more charged. More aware.

"Restless," he repeated, eyes roving her so thoroughly she wondered what she looked like. Her hair teased along her bare shoulder, her silk nightdress suddenly feeling very insubstantial, even though the blanket covered her breasts.

Images from her dream flitted back into her mind,

and she bit her lip as her gaze moved down his face, to his hands reaching up to her exposed shoulders. Looking back at him through her eyelashes, she could tell he sensed the charged atmosphere, too. But his hands didn't move. Not as she'd expected—and wanted—them to. There was something else besides hunger in the way he held her gaze. Something that looked a bit like worry.

"Gervais, I truly am all right. But are *you* all right?"

He ran his hand through the hair on top of his head, eyes turning glossy and unfocused. "I called my dad tonight to tell him about the pregnancy. Not the twin part. Just…that he's going to be a grandfather. I didn't want him to hear it in the news."

She thought of how the day had gone so crazy so fast simply because she passed out. "I wish we could have told your family together."

"You didn't include me when you told your family."

She looked away, guilt stinging her. And didn't that cool the heat that had been singeing her all over?

"You've told your family, haven't you?" he asked, his eyes missing nothing.

"I will. Soon. I know I have to before it hits the news." She wanted to change the subject off her family. Fast. "What did your family have to say? Your brothers were quiet at the emergency room."

"My brothers are all about family. No one judges. We love babies."

Erika raised her eyebrows, unsure how to take the casual tone of what felt like a very serious conversation. She noticed he didn't include his father in that last part.

"That is all?" she asked, knowing she had no right

to quiz him when she hadn't shared much about her own family.

"That's it. Now we need to tell your parents before they find out."

"I realize that."

"I want to be with you, even if it's on the phone in a Skype session." His jaw flexed in a way she was beginning to recognize—a surefire sign of determination. He slid his arms around her and said, "I want to reassure them I plan to marry their daughter."

Seven

"You have forgotten we have *no* plans to get married. I have plans—other plans. Our plans are in flux."

Erika pulled out of Gervais's arms so fast he damn near fell off the bed. He wasn't sure why he'd raised the issue again, other than not wanting to be like his father, and certainly the timing of his proposal hadn't been the smoothest. But the least she could do was consider it, since they hadn't taken time to seriously discuss it that first night.

Time to change that now. He shifted on the bed so they were face-to-face. And promptly remembered how little she must be wearing under that blanket. A bare shoulder peeked above the fabric, calling his hands to rake the barrier down and away.

To slide between those covers with her.

"Why not even consider?" he ground out between clenched teeth, determined to stay on track with this talk. "We have babies on the way. Even if we have a civil ceremony and stay together for the children's first year." From the scowl on her beautiful face he could see he was only making this worse. "Erika?"

"I came here to tell you about being pregnant, see if you want to be an active father, and then make plans from there. I didn't come for a yearlong repeat of our impulsive weekend together."

He swallowed. Had his carnal thoughts been that obvious? No sense denying that he wanted her.

"And what would be so wrong with that?"

"I have a life in another country."

"You're out of the military now. So work here. You have more job flexibility than I do."

Red flushed into her cheeks, making her look more like a shield maiden and less like a delicate princess in need of saving. "You are serious?"

The more he thought about it, the more it felt right. A marriage of convenience for a couple of years. He stroked her hair back and tucked it behind her ear, the silky strands gliding along his fingers. "We have amazing chemistry. We have children on the way. You're already staying in my home—"

"For two weeks," she said, finality edging her voice.

"Why not longer? Things have changed now with the twins. Two babies at once would be a lot for anyone to care for."

He needed to be involved. A part of his children's lives.

"I have plans for this fall. A commitment to my career. You are thinking too far into the future." She shook her head, a toss of silvery-blond hair in the moonlight. "Please slow down."

She angled an elbow against a bolster pillow, reclining even as she remained seated. And damn, but he wanted to be the one she leaned against, the one who supported her incredible body through the upcoming months while she carried this burden for them.

"We don't have that option for long. And you yourself said you were concerned about the babies being boys and being caught up in the family monarchy as next in line. If they're born here and we're married here in the States…" He wasn't exactly sure what that would mean for the monarchy, but it certainly would slow things down. Give them time to become a family. And to figure out how everything would work together.

She clapped a hand over his mouth. "Stop. Please. I cannot make this kind of decision now."

The magnolia scent of her lotion caught him off guard. He breathed in the scent, enjoying the cool press of her skin on his lips. Would have said as much if he hadn't noticed the glimmer of tears in her eyes.

A raggedy breath before speaking. "Can we please think about our future rationally? When I am rested and more prepared?" Though she did her best to look past him, every inch a regal monarch in that moment, he could see the strain in her cheeks.

She'd had a helluva long day. Fainted. Found out she was pregnant with twins. And she still had not gotten her damn chili dog.

There was a lot going on.

He could cut her some slack, give her space to collect herself. It was no use pushing so hard while she was emotional. And she had every right to be. Hell, he'd been upset tonight, too, uncharacteristically irritated with his father.

So he would revise his approach until cooler heads prevailed. This tactic to get her to stay was not the right one. She'd dismissed it out of hand.

Who could blame her, though? He'd given her no real reason to stay. And, as much as he hated to admit it, Erika Mitras was a woman who did not need him for anything. She could afford the best care and doctors for her pregnancy the same as he could. She would have highly qualified help with day-to-day care in her homeland.

But what she hadn't realized yet was that they were so damn good together. There was something between them, a small spark that could be more. And they had the children to consider.

Rather than insist she stay, he'd convince her. Which meant she was in for some grade A romancing. That was something he could give her that she couldn't just find in a store.

He would win her the old-fashioned way. Because like hell if he was losing his children. Missing out on the lives of his offspring simply wasn't an option. He'd make sure of that.

The next evening Erika still could not make sense of what had happened the night before. But no matter which way she spun Gervais's actions in her bed last night, nothing made sense. She'd been so sure that he wanted her. That he felt that same sharp tug of attraction between them, but his decision to simply walk away and let her go to bed alone had left her surprised. Confused. Aching. Wanting.

He hadn't mentioned the baby issue at all the whole day, then he surprised her with this dinner date, a night out in the city they called the Big Easy.

Draping an arm along the white-painted wrought-iron railing of the patio, her hand kept time to the peppy jazz music playing. She hadn't realized her head nodded along to the trumpet until Gervais flashed her a smile.

Heat flushed her cheeks as she turned her attention away from the very attractive man in front of her. She pushed around the last bite of her shrimp and andouille sausage, a spicy blend of flavors she'd quizzed their waiter about at length. Every course of her meal had been delicious.

Attention snapping to the present, she caught a whiff of something that smelled a lot like baked chocolate and some kind of fruit. Maybe cherries, but she couldn't be sure. All she knew was that her senses were heightened lately.

As were her emotions.

What was Gervais up to with this perfect evening? Was he trying to charm her into changing her mind without discussing the logistical fact that he still moved too fast?

Setting her fork down, she inclined her head to the meal. "Dinner was lovely. Thank you."

His dark eyes slid over her. One forearm lay on the crisp white linen tablecloth, his tanned hand close to where hers rested. He made her breath catch, and she felt sure she was not the only woman in the vicinity who was affected. She liked that he didn't notice. That his gaze was only for her.

"I'm glad you enjoyed yourself. But the evening doesn't have to end now." His hand slid closer to hers on the table.

Her tummy flipped. Did he mean—

Standing, he folded her palm in his. "Let's dance."

She was relieved, right?

Oh, heavens, she was a mess.

She took his hand, the warmth of his touch steadying her as he guided her over to the small teak dance floor. Briefly they were waylaid by an older couple who congratulated Gervais on the Hurricanes' win the day before. But while he was gracious and polite, he didn't linger, keeping his attention on her.

On their date and this fairy-tale evening that Gervais had created for her.

Beneath the tiny, gem-colored pendants, he pulled her into him as the slow, sultry jazz saxophone bayed. With ease, his right hand found the small of her back, and his left hand closed around her hand. As they began to sway, he tucked her against him, chest to chest underneath the din of the music and the lights.

The scents and sounds were just a colorful blur, though, her senses attuned to Gervais. The warm heat of his body through his soft silk suit. His fingers flexing lightly on her back, his thumb grazing bare skin where a cutout in her dress left her exposed.

She swallowed. Each fast breath of air she dragged in pressed her breasts to the hard wall of his chest, reminding her how well her body knew his. What would it be like to be with him now, with her senses so heightened? It had been incredible two and a half months ago.

She couldn't hold back a soft purr. She covered by saying, "The music is beautiful."

"It's the heartbeat of our city. The rhythm the whole place moves to."

He whirled her past the bass player, where the deep vibrations hummed right through her feet.

"There's so much more about my hometown to show you beyond our sports. So much history and culture here. And of course, some amazing food."

Which she could still smell drifting on the breeze. The scent of spices thickened the air, making the heat of the evening seem more exotic than any of the places she'd ever been to during her stint in the military.

"I cannot deny this Big Easy fascinates me." She could lose herself in these brick-and-wrought-iron-laced streets, the scent of flowers heavy in the air. "But I want to be clear, as much as I enjoyed the food tonight, or how much I might like the sound of jazz, that is not going to make me automatically change my mind about your proposal. We have nothing in common."

His voice tickled in her ear, a murmur accompanying the jazz quartet. "Sure we do. We both come from big families with lots of siblings."

A shiver trembled along her skin, and she reminded

herself it was just the pregnancy making her so suscep-
tible to him. It had to be. No man could mesmerize a
woman so thoroughly otherwise. Her hormones simply
conspired against her.

"I guess your family does qualify as American royalty." She held up her end of the conversation, hoping
he could not see the effect he had on her. "So that is
one thing we have in common. Just minus the crowns."

"True. No tiaras here." His head dipped closer to
speak in her ear again. "Although thinking of you in
a tiara and nothing more—that's an image to die for."

She knew he joked. That did not stop her from imag-
ining being naked with him.

"An image that will have to remain in your mind
only, since I do not pose for pictures. After what happened to my sister because of the sex tape with the
prime minister," she said, shuddering, "not a chance."

Gervais almost missed a step, though he recovered
quickly enough.

"Your sister was in a sex tape?"

"You must be the only person in the world who did
not see it." That snippet of footage had almost ruined
her family. The publicity was all the more difficult to
deflect, since their monarchy was both defunct and not
particularly wealthy. They'd had precious few resources
to fight with.

"Never mind." Gervais shook his head, dismiss-
ing that conversation. "That's beside the point. First, I
wasn't speaking literally. And second, I would never,
never let you be at risk that way."

Her neck craned to look at him, eyes scanning his

face. There was no amusement in her eyes. "Perhaps more to the point, I will not put myself at risk."

"You're an independent princess. I like that."

"Technically, I am a princess in name only. The monarchy doesn't have ruling power any longer."

"Fair enough."

Gervais spun her away from him. There was a moment before she returned to the heat of his body that left her with anticipation. She wanted him to keep touching her, to keep pressing his body against hers.

After they resumed their rhythmic swaying, he said softly into her ear, "You are pretty well-adjusted for someone who grew up in a medieval castle surrounded by servants and nannies."

"What makes you think we had servants and nannies?"

A smile played with his sexy mouth. "That princess title."

She rolled her eyes. "The castle was pretty crumbly and we had some maintenance help, since we opened part of the palace to the public, and tutors volunteered just to have it on their résumé that they'd taught royalty. But definitely no nannies."

"Your parents were the involved types." Somehow they had gotten closer, lips barely a breadth away from each other. The thought of how close he was made it hard for Erika to concentrate. So she pulled back a bit, adjusting her head to look out over the crowd, toward the band.

"Not really. After class we had freedom to roam. We were quite a wild pack of kids. Can you imagine having your own real-life castle as a playground? We had everything but the unicorn."

"You make it sound fun."

"Some days it was fun. Some it was lonely when I saw the kids on tour with their parents." She hesitated. The last thing she wanted from Gervais was sympathy. She'd accepted what her family was and was not a long time ago. So she continued, "And some days were downright dangerous."

"What do you mean?"

"My sisters and I wanted a trampoline for Christmas." Which sounded perfectly normal. Except for the Mitras clan, there was no such thing as normal.

"Okay. And?"

"You do not get those on royal grounds. It does not fit the historical image, and without the tours we didn't have money. So, we made our own."

"Oh, God." A look of horror and intrigue passed over his face.

"We pulled a couple of mattresses down the stairs, stacked them under a window... And we jumped."

Gervais's eyes widened. "From how high?"

She shrugged. "Third story. And the ceilings were high."

"You're making me ill."

"It was only scary the first time when one of my sisters pushed me." And, later, when another sister broke an arm and the game ended for good.

"Pushed you?" Disbelief filled his voice. Surely his brothers had done equally dangerous things as forms of entertainment when they had been younger.

She'd seen the Reynaud males up close, and there was an air of confidence and arrogance about all of them that didn't exactly coincide with a sheltered upbringing.

"I was the test dummy," she informed him. "As the youngest and the lightest, it was my job to make sure the mattress had been placed correctly and had enough bounce."

"And did it?"

"We had to add some duvets and pillows."

"So it hurt."

"Probably no more than playing football without shoulder pads."

Tucking a loose strand of her hair behind her ear, he whispered, "You're such a badass. I expected a story like that from a family of boys, but not girls."

Not all girls were the descendants of female warriors. And that was usually the justification for their shenanigans as children. "We considered it our gym class. It was more interesting than lacrosse."

"Lacrosse, huh? I didn't expect that." He brushed his lips across her temple, his breath warm, his brief kiss warmer.

Her body even warmer still with want.

Just when she thought she would grip his lapels and melt right into him, he stepped back.

"I should get you home, Princess. It's late."

And just like that, the fairy-tale book was closing. She felt close to him all evening, physical distance aside. And every time it seemed as if there was something more between them, he pulled back.

While part of her was relieved that he'd stopped pushing for more, a larger part of her wanted him. She had to weigh her options. Had to be strong for her unborn children and make the wisest decision possible. It wasn't just her life in the balance.

After a sleepless night dreaming of Gervais's touch, Erika hadn't awoken in the best of moods. And now she had to make the phone call she had been dreading. The one that had sent her on edge all morning long until she found her courage and started dialing.

Erika sat on the chaise longue in the guest room as she hugged the device to her ear and listened to the call ring through on the other side of the world. She needed to speak with her parents and tell them that she was pregnant. With twins. There was no sense in avoiding the inevitable any longer.

Her mother answered the phone. "Hello, my love. What brings about this lovely surprise of a call?"

"Um, does there have to be a special reason for me to call you?"

"There does not have to be, but I hear a tone in your voice that tells me there is a reason. Something important perhaps?"

Her mother's surprise intuition tugged at her already tumultuous emotions.

"I am pregnant. With twins." The words tumbled out of her mouth before she had even had a chance to respond to the pleasantries with her mom.

So much for the long speech Erika had outlined and perfected. Glancing down at the piece of paper in front of her, she noted that her talking points were basically for show. There was no going back now.

Silence fell from the other end of the receiver for what seemed like an eternity.

"Mother?" she asked, uncertainty creeping into her voice.

"Twins, Erika? Are you certain?"

She nodded, as if her mother could see. "Yes, Mother. I'm certain. I went to the doctor two days ago and heard the two distinct heartbeats with my own ears. The tradition of twins lives on in the Mitras family."

"Who is the father?" Her mother's interest pressed into the phone.

"Gervais Reynaud, the American football team owner—" she began, but her mother interrupted.

"A son of the Reynaud shipping empire? And Zephyr Cruise Ships? What an excellent match, Erika. American royalty. The press will love this."

"Right, but, Mother, I wanted to—"

"Oh, darling, have you considered what this could mean for the family? If you have boys, well…the royal line lives on. This is wonderful, my love. Hold on, let me get your father."

Rustling papers and some yelling came through over the phone. Erika's stomach knotted.

"Your father is on speakerphone. Tell him your news, my love." Her mother cooed into the phone, focused on all the wrong things.

"I'm going to have twins, Father. And I'm just—"

"Twins? Do you know what this means? You could have a boy. Maybe two."

Erika nodded dully into the phone, the voices of her parents feeling distant. As if they belonged in someone else's life. The way they had when she was a child. The image of the royal family always seemed more important than the actual well-being of the family itself.

They weren't interested in hearing what she had to say but were already strategizing how to best monetize this opportunity. The press was about to have an all-access pass to her life before she even knew how she was going to proceed.

"Mother, Father," she said, interrupting their chatter, "I've had quite the morning already." They didn't need to know how much it taxed a woman to daydream about Gervais just when he'd decided to pull back. "Do you mind if I call you later, after I've rested?"

Tears burned her eyes for a variety of reasons that shouldn't make her cry. Pregnancy hormones were pure evil.

"Of course not, my love."

"Not at all, my dear," her father said. "You need your rest if you are going to raise the future of the royal line. Sleep well."

And just like that, they were gone, leaving her cell phone quiet as the screen went dark. They had disconnected from the call as abruptly as they often did from her life, leaving her all alone to contend with the biggest challenge she'd ever faced.

"Well, we're surprised to see you so early, that's all," Dempsey said from a weight bench, his leg propped up on a stool. He pressed around his knee, fidgeting with the brace. An old injury that had cost him his college football career. It was flaring up again. Most days, it didn't bother him. But then there were days like today.

Gervais understood Dempsey's position. He'd been sidelined from the field, as well. One too many concussions. But quite frankly, he enjoyed the business side of owning the Hurricanes.

There were new challenges, new ways of looking at the game and new styles of offense to develop as players came up stronger and faster than ever before. And he was still involved in football, which had been his ultimate goal anyway. This had just been another way to get at the same prize.

As an owner, he would not only strategize how to field the best possible team, he would also make the Hurricanes the most profitable team in the league. Corporate sponsorships were on track to meet that goal in three years, but Gervais had plans that could shorten that window to two. Maybe even eighteen months. The franchise thrived and the city along with it.

"I'm not sure what you two find so fascinating about my night out with Erika." Gervais curled the dumbbells, sweat starting to form on his brow as they worked out in a private facility within the team's training building.

The team lifted in a massive room downstairs, but Gervais had added a more streamlined space upstairs near the front offices.

"We just want to know what's going on in your life. With the baby. And you," Henri, their father's favorite, added. Theo had high hopes that Henri would one day wear a Super Bowl ring for the Hurricanes and continue in the old man's footsteps as a hometown hero.

The whole family was here, with the exception of their father and their brother Jean-Pierre, who played for a rival team in New York and didn't get to Louisiana much during the season.

And while Henri technically worked out with the team, he never minded putting in some extra hours in the upstairs training center to try to show up his older brothers in the weight room.

"That offer still stands, by the way, if you want it to," Henri said, his voice low enough so only Gervais could hear. Gervais knew that things had been hard for Henri and his wife since they hadn't been able to conceive. It affected everything in their marriage. But Gervais wasn't about to give them his unborn children. He wanted to raise them, to be an active part of their lives. To be the opposite of their father.

"Hey now, secrets don't make friends," Dempsey snapped, his face hard. Henri rolled his eyes but nodded anyway.

"So, Pops—" Dempsey shot him an amused grin "—have you decided what you are going to do?"

"Yeah, how are you going to handle fatherhood in the public eye with a princess?" Henri teased, huffing out pull-ups on a raised bar.

"I told you both, I'm taking care of my children." And Erika, he added silently. His main goal as they got ready for the game in St. Louis was to show her that they could be together. That they were great together. An unconventional family that could beat the odds. He was prepared to romance her like no other. And he might have shared that with Henri and Dempsey, if not for the man that rounded the corner, stopping in the entrance to the weight room.

From the door frame, a familiar booming drawl. Theo. "I'm here to meet the mother of my first grandchild."

Eight

As the limo driver faded from view, Erika sped into the Hurricanes' office building. She moved as fast as her legs would carry her, feeling less like royalty and more like a woman on a mission.

Twenty minutes ago, Gervais had called her. Urgency flooded his voice. He needed her in the office stat.

Pushing the heavy glass door open, she took a deep breath, feeling ever so slightly winded. The humidity was something she had yet to fully adjust to, and even small stints outside left her vaguely breathless. The rush of the cool air-conditioning filled her lungs as she crossed the threshold, a welcome chill after the New Orleans steam bath. Striding beneath the black-and-gold team banners hanging overhead, she struggled to figure out what was wrong that he needed her here.

Taking the stairs two at a time, she made it to the second floor and hung a right. Headed straight for the glass wall and door with an etched Hurricanes logo.

The secretary smiled warmly at her from her desk. Adjusting her glasses, she stood. "Princess Erika, Mr. Reynaud is expecting you—"

Extending a manicured hand, she gestured to another door and Erika didn't wait for her to finish. Hurrying forward, she reached the polished double doors made of a dark wood. And heavy. She gave one side a shove, practically falling into the huge office of the team owner.

Currently an empty room.

Erika looked around, heart pounding with nerves. And, if she was being honest, disappointment.

Spinning on her heel, she practically ran into the secretary. Grace was not on her side today.

"My apologies, ma'am," the secretary started in a quiet voice. "Mr. Reynaud will be back in a few minutes, but please make yourself comfortable. Can I get you anything while you wait? We have water, soda, tea. And of course enough Gatorade to fill a stadium."

"Thank you." As the words left her lips, she settled down. Slightly. "I'm just fine, though."

"Of course." The secretary smiled, exiting the room and closing the door with a soft click.

So she was here. In his office without him. While not ideal, it did give her a chance to feel out what sort of man he was. At least in the business sense.

A bank of windows overlooked the practice field below, the lush green grass perfectly manicured with the white gridiron standing out in stark contrast. Silver bleachers glimmered all around the open-air facility with a retractable dome. Funny they didn't have the stadium roof on today when it was so beastly hot outside, but perhaps the practice had been earlier in the day as there were no players in sight now.

Turning from the wall of windows, she paced around the office. She noted the orderly files, the perfectly straightened paper stacks on the massive mahogany desk. The rows of sticky notes by the phone. The walls were covered with team photos and awards, framed press clippings and a couple of leather footballs behind glass cases. The place was squared away. Tight.

Not too different from the way she kept her own living quarters, either. Impersonal. Spit-shined for show. They might not have done a lot of talking in London, but clearly they had gravitated toward each other for reasons beyond the obvious. After last night she felt as if they had more in common than they realized.

A tightness worked in her chest. So desperately did she want to trust him now that they found themselves preparing to be parents together. But trust came at a high cost. It wasn't a commodity she candidly bestowed. It was earned—her most guarded asset. Years of being royalty had taught her to be suspicious.

Shoving her past aside, she approached a picture on the farthest corner of his desk. It was different than the rest. It seemed to have nothing to do with the Hurricanes. Or football, for that matter.

The photograph was faded, old—probably real film instead of digital. But she would have recognized him anyway. Gervais. His brothers. A woman. His mother, she assumed. But no Dempsey. Which struck her as odd.

She would have continued to stare at the picture as if it could give her the answers she was after if she didn't hear a man clearing his throat behind her.

She glanced over her shoulder, through the blond strands of her hair. Gervais stood in the doorway. And he looked damn sexy.

He was disheveled. Not nearly as put together as his office. His hair was still wet from a shower, and his shirt was only half buttoned. For the quickest moment she had the urge to finish undoing it. To kiss him—and more.

The urge honestly surprised her. She had promised herself yesterday that after a good night's sleep, she would be levelheaded today. She needed logic to prevail while she figured out if he could be trusted. Only then could she decide what to do next.

Leaning against the desk, and looking at his lips with feigned disinterest, she asked as casually as possible, "What is the emergency? Is something wrong?"

He shook his head, closing the door behind him. "Not really. I just wanted to speak with you privately about—" he hesitated "—a…uh…new development."

Her smile faded. He was leaving. People always did. Her parents, who never remained in town with their kids for long. The vast majority of her friends who hung around only because she was royalty. The dozens of tutors who only helped for long enough to get a good reference before moving on to an easier job than five hell-raising sisters.

Schooling her features to remain impassive, she sat

down in a leather wingback chair. She needed the isolation that chair represented. She didn't need him tempting her by sitting next to her on the sofa or walking up to her to brush against her. Touch her. Weaken her resolve.

"Tell me." She met his gaze. Steeled herself.

"Remember that I told you I called my father a couple of days ago to tell him about the baby?" His dark eyes found hers for a moment before he stalked toward the wall of windows and looked down at the field. "Apparently, he decided to make a surprise visit."

"Your father is here? In the building or in New Orleans?"

The tight feeling in her chest returned, seizing hold of her. Erika was as unsure of how to deal with his family as she was her own. Selfishly, she had hoped they would have alone time together—without family making plays and demands—to figure out how to handle their situation. And to figure out if there was something there between them, after all.

"He was in the building but he's taking his girlfriend out to lunch before coming to the house later. I wanted to warn you in person and couldn't leave work."

More confirmation she didn't want to hear. But she felt compelled to hear it anyway. "Why do I need warning?"

"He's not a good person in spite of being charming as hell when he wants to be. I just want to make sure you're prepared. Feel free to steer clear of him."

"I can take care of myself. If he becomes too much to handle, I will flip him with Krav Maga I learned in the military." The warrior blood boiled beneath her skin. She would not be taken for a fool.

"You're pregnant."

"I am not incapacitated. But if you are concerned, I will simply pretend I do not understand his English." Uncrossing her arms, she gave him a wickedly innocent grin. Eyes wide for full effect. "It worked on almost half the tutors who showed up at the Mitras household prepared to teach the rebellious princesses."

"Good plan. Wish I'd thought of that as a kid."

A laugh escaped him and he turned toward her, a good-natured smile pushing at his cheeks. Funny how that smile slid right past her resolve to let logic prevail. To be levelheaded. That shared laugh stirred a whole wealth of feelings that had been building inside her ever since she'd stepped onto the practice field to face Gervais Reynaud.

Thinking back to the photograph on the desk, she had to admit, she was curious about him. His past. What it was like growing up in New Orleans. She had so many things to learn about him that it could take a lifetime. And wasn't it perfectly *reasonable* of her to learn more about him when her children would share his genes?

Emboldened by the rationalization, she thought she might as well begin her quest to know him better right now. "But you did not need to arm yourself with elaborate schemes to outwit the grown-ups around you as a child. You and your brothers are so close—or the three of you I've met."

The faintest pull of unease touched his lips. "We weren't always. Dempsey didn't come to live with us until he was thirteen. Our dad… Maybe you already know this."

"No, I do not."

"That's right." He shifted away from the windows to move closer to her, taking a seat on the edge of the desk. "You're not a big follower of football and the players."

"I am learning to be. You make me curious about anything that relates to you." Leaning forward, she touched his arm gently.

"I'm glad." A small victory. She could see him struggling with his family history, despite the fact that it was, apparently, public knowledge.

"Why did Dempsey come to live with you later?"

"We have different mothers."

"Your parents got divorced? But—" That certainly did not seem strange.

He met her gaze, his expression tight. "The ages don't match up. I'm the oldest, then Dempsey, followed by Henri and Jean-Pierre. Dad slept around on Mom, a lot."

"Gervais, I am so very sorry." She touched his arm lightly, which was as much sympathy as she dared offer without risking him pulling away or shutting down.

"My father used to go to clubs with his friends. Remember, this was before the internet made it possible to stalk your date before you'd ever met." He took another breath, clearly uncomfortable.

Erika's eyes widened, realizing that he was opening up to her.

"All families have…dead bones in the closet," she said quietly.

A smile pushed against his lips. "You mean skeletons?"

"Is that not the same thing?" She ran her hand over his.

"More or less, I suppose. Anyway, he hooked up with Dempsey's mom, Yvette, at a jazz club. She got pregnant. Worked a lot of jobs to raise Dempsey, but never found my father, since he hadn't even been honest about who he was, apparently. Until his image was blasted all over the sports page and she recognized his face. Yvette thought it was her ticket out of the slums. She arranged a meeting with my father. But he insisted Dempsey become part of the family. And Dempsey's mother agreed. For a price."

How horrible for Dempsey. And, from Gervais's perspective, how horrible it must have been for him to assimilate a new brother almost his own age when they were both young teens. She avoided focusing on him, however, guessing he would only shift gears if she did.

"That had to be strange for your mother," she observed lightly.

He bit back a bark of a laugh. "Strange? She wasn't much of a motherly type. After one more kid got added to the mix, she left."

"That is so much change for children." Her heart swelled with sympathy for him. She had no idea that there was so much struggle in the Reynaud family.

"We didn't handle it well. I was jealous. Henri was my shadow, so he followed my lead. We blamed Dempsey for breaking up our parents, which was ridiculous from an adult perspective. But kids can be cruel."

"What happened?"

He looked at her sidelong. "We were living in Texas then. Staying at our grandfather's ranch while our father chased our mother around, trying to work things out. Anyway, I dared Dempsey to ride a horse. The biggest, meanest horse on the ranch."

"Oh, my."

"You don't sound horrified."

She shrugged her shoulders. "Remember? My sisters threw me out a third-story window. I know how siblings treat each other even when they have grown up together."

"True enough." He nodded. "Of course, he had no idea how to ride—not even a nice horse. So he was… completely unprepared for a high-strung Thoroughbred used to getting her own way."

"That's scary. What happened?"

"She threw him clear off, but he landed awkwardly and broke his leg. We both almost got trampled while Henri and Jean-Pierre ran to get help."

"You did not mean to break his leg." Ah, sibling cruelty was something that existed in all countries.

"Things were difficult between us for a long while, even once we all made up. I don't want my children to live in a fractured family. Not if I can help it. I want them to have a firm sense of belonging, a sense of being a Reynaud."

"And a Mitras," she reminded him.

"Yes. Both." He reached out to take her hands in his and squeezed. "I want your strength in our children. They will need it."

His words warmed her even more than his touch, and that was saying a lot when a thrill danced over her skin.

Too breathless to answer, she bit her lip, unwilling to allow a dreamy sigh to escape.

"Erika, please stay here with me for a while. We need more time to get to know each other." He drew her to her feet, his eyes pleading with hers at a time when her resolve was at an all-time low.

Her heart beat wildly, her lips parted. Anticipating the press of his mouth to hers.

He rubbed her arms, sliding them up until his hands tangled in her hair. They kissed deeply, with open mouths and passion. Tendrils of desire pulsed through her as he explored her mouth with his tongue, tasting her as she tasted him right back. She had not been passive in their lovemaking before, and she could already feel the urge to seize control driving her to the brink now.

It could have gone on like that for hours, for days even, if not for the sound of the door opening. She pushed back. Looked down. Away. At anything else but him.

While Gervais spoke in a low voice to his secretary, Erika used the time to collect herself. Straighten her dress. Find her purse. She had to figure this out soon. It was apparent there was chemistry simmering hot just beneath the surface. But now there was also a tenderness of feeling. An emotional connection. How would she ever forget that look in Gervais's eyes when he told her about the guilt of seeing Dempsey hurt? Of course she understood why he wanted to keep his own family intact. His children connected.

That was admirable, and a deeper draw for her than the sensual spell he cast around her without even trying. It had been difficult enough resisting just one.

How would she ever keep her wits about her with both those persuasive tools at his disposal?

On the private plane to St. Louis later that week, Erika replayed the kiss in Gervais's office over and over again. Of course, she had already relived that moment in her mind more than once, awake and asleep. Every look between them was filled with so much steam she could barely think, much less trust herself to make logical decisions around him.

At least they were on different planes today, so she could avoid temptation for a few hours. All the wives and girlfriends traveled first-class, while the team went on a chartered craft. Gervais had a meeting in Chicago first, something to do with corporate sponsorship for the Hurricanes. But he would arrive in St. Louis at the same time she did.

With any luck, she could use this flight to get her bearings straight.

But even as she tried to focus on being objective, her mind wandered back to the kiss in the office. A kiss that hadn't been repeated despite the fact that they'd spent time together over the past few days. It felt as though he was always on the clock, managing something for the team or overseeing business for one of the other Reynaud family concerns. So he was a bit of a workaholic; not a flaw in her opinion. In fact, she respected how seriously he took his work. He expected nothing to be handed to him in life.

And when they were together, he was fully present. Attentive. Thoughtful. He'd even helped deflect an awkward run-in with his father and his father's girl-friend because she hadn't felt ready to face Theo after what she'd learned about him. And knowing how little his own son trusted him.

Erika's instincts had seldom failed her. In London, there had been something between them. Something she hadn't imagined. And the more she thought about the past few days, the more excited she was to be with him again. To have another kiss. To throw away caution as quickly as clothes peeled away in the heat of passion.

To make love again and discover if the fire burned as hot between them as she remembered.

Erika clutched a long silver necklace in her hand, running the charm back and forth. Just as she did as a child.

Fiona, Henri's wife, gently touched her arm. "You know, we have a book club to help pass the time when we're on the road with the guys."

"A book club?" She glanced at the row across from her, to where Gervais's father's girlfriend stared intently at a fashion magazine.

Fiona scrunched her nose. "I should have asked. Do you like to read?"

"Which language?"

Fiona laughed lightly. "No need to get all princess-sy on me."

"I apologize. That was meant to be a joke. Sometimes nuances, even though I speak all those languages, get lost. Tell me more about the book club."

"We choose books to read during all those flights

and then we have one helluva party while we discuss them."

"Party?"

Fiona nodded. "Spa or five-star restaurant or even the best room service we can buy."

"Did Gervais ask you to sit here and use the time to convince me it is fun to be on the road?" Try as she might, Erika couldn't keep the dry sarcasm out of her voice.

"I am simply helping you make an informed decision. It's not just about partying. We have homeschooling groups for families with children, as well." Shadows passed briefly through her eyes before Fiona cleared her throat. "It's amazing what you can teach a child when your field trips involve traveling around the country. Even overseas sometimes for the preseason. Our kids have bonds, too. There are ways to make this kind of family work. Family is important."

Damn. That struck a chord with her. Maybe Fiona had a point. She had just dismissed the women of the group without bothering to really get to know them. And that certainly was not fair.

Maybe she could strengthen her ties to Gervais's world this way. She already knew she wanted to explore their relationship more thoroughly—to take that first step of trust with him and see where indulging their sensual chemistry would lead. But in the meantime, why not work on forging bonds within his world? If things between them didn't work and they ended up co-parenting on opposite sides of the world, she would need allies in the Reynaud clan and in the Hurricanes organization. Growing closer to Fiona would be a good thing for her children.

All perfectly logical.

Except that a growing part of Erika acknowledged she wasn't just thinking about a rational plan B anymore. With each day that passed, with every moment that she craved Gervais, Erika wanted plan A to work. And that meant this trip was going to bring her much closer to the powerful father of her children.

There was nothing Gervais hated more than a loss. It rubbed him the wrong way, sending him into a dark place, even though he knew that a preseason loss didn't matter. The preseason was about training. Testing formations. Trying out new personnel. The final tally on the score sheet didn't count toward anything meaningful.

Opening the door to his suite, he was taken aback by what he saw on the bed. Erika in a Hurricanes jersey. On her, it doubled as a dress, hitting her midthigh. Exposing her toned legs.

His mind eased off the loss, focused on what was in front of him. "I wanted to catch you before you went to bed."

She closed the book she'd been reading and uncurled her legs, stretching them out on the bed. "I am sorry about the game."

"I won't lie. I'm disappointed we lost this one. But I'm realistic enough to know we can't win every time, especially in the preseason when we don't play all of our starters or utilize our best offensive strategies. The whole point of the preseason is like a testing ground.

We can create realistic scenarios and see what happens when we experiment." He told himself as much, but it didn't soothe him when he saw a rookie make poor decisions on the field or watched a risky play go up in flames.

"You have a cool head. That is admirable."

Her head tilted sympathetically.

Gervais was floored. Unsure of what to make about Erika's behavior. For the first time since her arrival in the United States, it felt as if she was opening up to him. But could that be?

She'd been so adamant on keeping distance between them, urging logic over passion. She was probably just being polite to him. After all, they would have to be civil to each other for the sake of the children. She had said as much more than once.

Still, damn it, he knew what he saw in her eyes, and she wanted him every bit as much as he wanted her. Back in his arms.

In his bed.

"Thank you. I'm sorry I've been so busy the past few days." He had taken a red-eye to Chicago to be there this morning for a meeting to secure a new corporate sponsor for the team. He was exhausted, but the extra hours had paid off, and he was one step closer to making the Hurricanes the wealthiest team in the league.

"You have been very thoughtful." She leaned forward, her posture open, words unclipped.

Her gaze was soft on him. And appreciative, he noticed. So maybe he hadn't been so off base. "I was concerned you would feel neglected having to fly in a separate plane."

"I understand you have other commitments. And I had a lovely conversation with Fiona—in case you were wondering, since you made sure we had seats beside each other." Erika raised her eyebrows as if daring him to deny it.

"Are you angry?" He couldn't help that he wanted to give her reasons to stay in New Orleans. But he knew she did not appreciate being manipulated.

He'd never met a more independent woman.

"Actually, no. She was helpful in explaining the logistics of how wives blend in to the lifestyle of this team you own."

He hadn't expected that.

"She answered all of your questions?"

"Most…" Shifting on the bed, she crawled toward him. "I had cats when I grew up."

All of his exhaustion disappeared.

His eyes couldn't help but watch her lithe form, the way her breasts pushed against the jersey he'd given her. An unforgettable vision.

And the sensory overload left him dumbly saying, "Okay."

"We had dogs, too, but the cats were mine."

Trying his damnedest to pull his eyes up from the length of her exposed legs, he stumbled over the next sentence, too. Focusing on words was hard. And he had thought that tonight's loss had left him speechless. That was nothing compared to the sight in front of him. "Um, what were their names?"

Erika's lips plumped into a smile as she knelt on the bed in front of him. "You do not need to work this hard or pretend to woo me."

"I'm not pretending. I am interested in everything about you." And he was. Mind, spirit…and body. He tried to keep his mind focused on the conversation. On whatever she wanted to talk about.

"Then you will want to know the real reason why I mentioned the cats. I loved my cats. And yet my children—our children—will not be able to have pets when they are traveling all over the country to follow this team that is part of their legacy." She gave him a playful shove, her smile still coy.

"Actually, I have a baseball buddy whose wife travels with her dog." He deserved a medal for making this much conversation when she looked like that. "I think the guy renegotiated his contract to make sure she got to have her dog with her."

"Oh," Erika whispered breathily. Moved closer to him, hands resting on his arms. Sending his body reeling from her touch.

"Yes, oh. So what other questions went unanswered today? Bring it. Because I'm ready."

"I do have one more question I did not dare to ask your sister-in-law." Her hands slid up to his neck. Pulled him close. Whispered with warm breath into his ear. "Will it mess up your season mojo if we have sex?"

Nine

Erika's heart hammered, threatening to fall right out of her chest as she stared at Gervais. All the time on the plane and waiting for him tonight had led her here. To this moment. And while the direction of her life may have been still uncertain, she knew this was right.

This was exactly where she needed to be. There was a closeness between them, one she had been actively fighting against.

Gervais's eyebrows shot upward. "What brought on this change?"

"I desire you. You want me, too, if I am not mistaken." Direct. Cool. She could do this.

"You are not mistaken. I have always wanted you. From the moment I first saw you. Even more now."

"Then we should stop denying ourselves the one

thing that is uncomplicated between us." And it was the truth. Everything was happening so fast, but it was undeniable that there was an attraction between them. In her gut, she knew that he would be there to support their babies. But it was more than that.

It was a deeper connection between them. When she had boarded the plane for New Orleans, she hadn't expected much from him. People had a nasty habit of leaving her, using her for the minimal privileges her royal status awarded her. She'd never expected to be welcomed and treated so well. In the past, her friends were dazzled by the idea of her world, rarely seeing beyond the outer trappings to the person beneath.

She also hadn't thought his family would be so accepting. It had scared her a bit, how many people were in the Reynaud clan. The number of people suddenly fussing over her and trying to get to know her had been overwhelming.

But they had also been kind. And maybe, just maybe, she'd be able to see past her preconceived notions about family. She had no real idea how to make a family anyway. But with Gervais...

"You're sure?" His forehead furrowed as he scrutinized her face. The look said everything. This was as far as he'd go without confirmation from her.

"Completely certain." She wanted to take a chance on him. On them. To give them an opportunity to be a couple.

And now that she'd made the decision after careful reasoning, she could finally allow her emotions to surface. She felt all her restraints melting away in the heat of the passion she'd been denying.

Even as she felt those walls disintegrate, she could sense a shift in Gervais. Like shedding a jacket and tie, he seemed to set aside his controlled exterior as a look of pure male desire flashed through his gaze. He closed the distance between them, his brown eyes dark and hungry while he raked his gaze over her.

He peeled the jersey up and over her head. She shook her hair free in waves that fanned behind her, leaving her rounded breasts bared to his devouring gaze. Heat pulsed through her veins—and relief. She had missed him since their incredible time together two and a half months ago, and she'd worked so hard to keep her desire for him in check for the sake of her babies so that she could make a smart decision where he was concerned. Now it felt so amazing to let go of those fears and simply fall into him.

She'd wondered what he would think of the subtle changes pregnancy had brought to her body. Her full breasts had fit in his palms before; now she knew they would overflow a hint more.

But Gervais's eyes were greedier for her than ever, and he stared at her with need he didn't bother to hide. Lowering her to rest on her back, he followed her down to the bed, his touch gentle but firm. His woodsy scent familiar and making her ache for him.

He hooked his thumbs in the sides of her pale blue panties, tugging gently until she raised her hips to accommodate. He slipped the scrap of satin down and off, flinging it aside to rest on top of the discarded Hurricanes jersey. His throat moved in a slow gulp. "That incredible image will be seared in my brain for all time."

He rocked back for a moment, his eyes roving over her.

Then his gaze fell to rest on the ever so slight curve of her stomach. The pregnancy was still early, but now she realized that the twins had been the reason her pants had grown a little snug faster than she would have expected.

A glint of protectiveness lit his eyes. "Are you sure this is safe? You passed out just last week. I don't want to do anything that could risk your health."

She thought she might die if he did not touch her, actually. But she kept that thought locked away.

"The doctor said I am healthy and cleared for all activities, including sex. Well, as long as we do not indulge in acrobatics." A wicked memory flashed through her brain. "Perhaps we should not re-create that interlude on the kitchen table in your London hotel room."

His heart slugged hard against his chest. Against hers. She wanted to arch into his warmth like a cat seeking the sun.

"No acrobatics. Understood." He trailed kisses beneath her ear and down her neck. "I look forward to treating you like spun glass."

A shiver tripped down her spine, her skin tingling with awareness. Tingles of heat gathered between her legs, making her long for more. For everything.

"I will not break," she promised, needing the pleasure only he could bring her.

He skimmed a fingertip down the length of her neck.

"Oh, careful, light touches can be every bit as arousing as our more aggressive weekend together."

She licked her lips. Swallowed over her suddenly dry throat.

"I look forward to your persuasion—once you take those clothes off." She ran her hands down his chest and back up his shoulders. "Because, Gervais…" She savored the feel of his name on her tongue. "You are seriously overdressed for the occasion. Undress for me."

His brown eyes went molten black with heat at her invitation, and his hands went to work on his tie, loosening the knot and tugging the length free, slowly, then draping the silver length over the chaise at the end of the bed. And oh my, how she enjoyed the way he took his time. One fastening at a time, he opened his white button-down until it flapped loose, revealing his broad, muscled chest in a T-shirt. In a deliberate motion he swept both aside and laid them carefully over his tie.

Her mouth went moist and she bit her bottom lip. She recalled exactly why she hadn't bothered with light, teasing touches the last time they were together. His body was so powerful, his every muscle honed. She hadn't been able to hold herself back the last time.

He winked at her with a playfulness that she didn't see in this intense man often.

She could not stop a wriggle of impatience, the Egyptian cotton sheets slick against her rapidly heating flesh.

Then all playfulness left his eyes as swiftly as he took off his shoes and pants, leaving his toned body naked and all for her.

The thick length of him strained upward against his

stomach. Unable to hold back, she sat up to run her hands up his chest, then down his sides, his hips, forward to clasp his steely strength in his hands. To stroke, again and again, teasing her thumb along the tip.

With a growl of approval and impatience, he stretched over her while keeping his full weight off her. He braced on his elbows, cupping her face and slanting his mouth along hers. His tongue filled her mouth and she knew soon, not soon enough, he would fill her body again.

His hands molded to her curves, exploring each of her erogenous zones with a perfection that told her he remembered every moment of their time together as much as she did. His hard thigh parted her legs, the firm pressure against her core sending her arching closer, wriggling against him, growing moist and needy. She clutched at his shoulders, breathy whispers sliding free as she urged him to take her. Now. No more waiting. He'd tormented her dreams long enough.

Then the blunt thickness of him pushed into her, inch by delicious inch. He was so gentle and strong at the same time. She knew she would have to be the one to demand more. Harder. Faster. And she did. With her words and body, rocking against him, her fingers digging into his taut ass to bring them both the completion they sought.

Her fingers crawled up his spine again and she pushed at his shoulders, nudging until he rolled to his back, taking her with him in flawless athleticism. His power, his strength, thrilled her. She straddled him, her sleek blond hair draped over her breasts, her nipples just peeking through and tightening. Gervais swept aside her hair and took one pink peak in his mouth. He circled with his tongue, sending bolts of pleasure radiating through her. Sighs of bliss slipped from between her lips. She rolled her hips faster, riding him to her completion. Wave after wave of her orgasm pulsed through her.

She heard his own hoarse shout of completion, the deep sounds sending a fresh wash of pleasure through her until she melted forward onto his chest. Sated. Every nerve tingling with awareness in the aftermath.

The swish of the ceiling fan sent goose bumps along her skin. The fine thread count of the sheets soothed her.

But most of all, the firm muscled length of him felt so good; the swirls of his body hair tempted her to writhe along him again.

If she could move.

And just like that, Erika realized how utterly complicated being with him was. Because like it or not, she had feelings for him. Feelings that were threatening to cloud her judgment.

And while this may have felt right for her, she needed to be sure it was right for him, too.

Gervais poured the flowery-scented shampoo into his hand. Her magnolia scent filled the steam and teased his senses as they stood under the shower spray in a vintage claw-foot tub. The sheer plastic curtain gave both privacy and a view of the room filled with fresh flowers he'd ordered sent up especially for her.

There was so very much he wanted to do for—and to—this incredible woman.

Drawing Erika close to him, he kissed her neck, nuzzled behind her ear, savored the wet satin of her skin against his bare flesh. Already he could feel the urge building inside him to lift her legs around his waist and surge inside her. To bring them both to completion again, but he was determined to take his time, to build the moment.

And yes, draw out the pleasure.

He lathered her hair, the bubbles and her hair slick between his fingers as he massaged her scalp. Her light moan of bliss encouraged him on, filling him with a sense of power over fulfilling all her needs. He continued to rub along her head, then gently along her neck, down to her shoulders in a slight massage. He wanted to pamper her, to show her he was serious about her and the babies.

She leaned into his touch but stayed silent. Feeling her let out a deep sigh, he decided he wanted to really get to know this beautiful, incredible woman. Sure, they'd spent some time together…but there was still so much he could learn about her. That he wanted to learn about *her*. Everything, not just about her beautiful body, but also about that magnificently brilliant mind of hers.

Such as why she had chosen a career in the military after growing up as royalty.

"So tell me about your time in the service. What did you really do?"

"Just what I told you that day we met."

"Truly? Nothing more? Not some secret spy role? Or dark ops career no one can ever know about?"

"How does the saying go in your country? I could tell you but then I would have to kill you."

He laughed softly against her mouth. "As long as we go while naked together, I'll die a happy man."

She swatted his butt playfully, then her smile faded. "Truthfully, there is nothing more to tell. I was a translator and handled some diplomacy meetings."

"I admire that about you." It had been a brave move. A noble, selfless act.

Shrugging, she tipped her shampooed head back into the water. Erika closed her eyes, clearly enjoying the feel of the steamy water. The suds caught on her curves, drawing his gaze. She was damn sexy.

"Why are you so dismissive of your service to your country?"

Eyes flashed open, defensive. He could tell it in the way she chewed on her lip before she answered, "I wanted to be a field medic and go into combat zones. But I was not allowed."

He nodded, trying to be sympathetic. To understand the complication of letting a princess, even from defunct royalty, into an active war zone.

"I can see how your presence could pose a security risk for those around you. You would be quite a high-value captive."

Her half smile carried a hint of cynicism. "While that is true, that was not the reason. My parents interfered. They did not want me to work or join at all. They wanted me to marry someone rich and influential, like I was some pawn in a royal chess game from a thousand years ago."

"Still, you made your own way. That's commendable. Why a field nurse and not in a military hospital?" He respected her drive. And her selfless career choices. She wanted to help people. Something told him she would have been a good field medic. Strong, knowledgeable, fearless.

"I did not want special treatment or protection because of my family's position. And still, I ended up as a translator not even allowed anywhere near a combat zone." Her voice took on a new determination. A tenacity he found incredibly attractive.

"So you made plans to continue your education after your service was finished." He knew she'd registered for coursework that would begin next month in the UK but had assumed she would ask for her spot to be held until after the children were born.

"I will not be deterred from my plans because of my family's interference." Eyes narrowed at him. Every bit a princess with that haughty stare. "I can support myself."

"Of course you can." He brought his negotiating skills to the conversation, hoping to make her see reason. "This is about more than money, though. You have a lot on your plate. Let me help you and the babies while you return to school."

"That makes it sound like I am incapable of taking care of myself the way my parents always said." Bitterness edged back into her voice. And something that sounded like dulled resignation.

"This isn't just about you. Or me. We have children to think of. You know I want you to marry me. I've made that clear. But if your answer is still no, at least move in with me. Make this easier for all—"

She pressed her mouth to his, silencing him until she leaned back, water dripping between them again.

"Gervais, please, this time is for us to get to know one another better. This kind of pressure from you about the future is counterproductive."

One thing was for sure—she had been opening up. Maybe asking her to marry him again was too much too soon. But he could feel the connection between them growing. So he would back off. But not forever. He just had to figure out a way to show her how good they were together. "Then how about we find food?"

Her smile was so gorgeous the water damn near steamed off his skin. "Food? Now that is music to this pregnant woman's ears."

The strands of Erika's hair fell damp against the cloth of the jersey. They sat in the suite's kitchen. She was on the countertop, cross-legged, peering over at Gervais's back.

He'd retrieved an assortment of ripe fruit—pitted cherries, chocolate-dipped strawberries, pineapple slices and peach slices. At the center of the platter was a bowl of indulgent-looking cream.

Stomach growling, she looked on in anticipation. He brought it next to her and pulled up a bar stool so that they were eye level.

Extending her hand to grab a cherry, he stopped her.

"Let me, Princess." With a playful smile, he lifted

a cherry to her lips. Inside, she felt that now-familiar heat pulse. He was tender, charming.

A threat to her plan of objectivity, too.

She popped a chocolate-dipped strawberry into his mouth. He licked the slightly melted chocolate off her fingertips, sending her mind back to the shower. Back to when she had thought this was uncomplicated.

Needing to take control of the situation, Erika cleared her throat. Her goal was the same as before. To get to know him. "What did you want to be as a little boy growing up?"

Finishing chewing, he tilted his head to the side. "Interesting question."

"How so?" It had seemed like a perfectly reasonable question. One she had been meaning to ask for a while now.

"Everyone assumes I wanted to be a pro football player."

To Erika, Gervais had seemed like the kind of man who wasn't nearly as cut-and-dried as that. He might live and breathe football, but it didn't seem as if it was the only dimension to him. Childhood dreams said a lot, after all. She'd wanted to be a shield maiden from long ago. To protect and shelter people. Her adult dream was still along those lines.

A nurse did such things. "And you did not want to be a football player like the rest of your family?"

"I enjoy the game. Clearly. I played all through elementary school into high school because I wanted to. I didn't have to accept the offer to play at the college level. I could afford any education I wanted."

"But your childhood dream?" She pressed on, before taking the cream-covered peach slice he'd offered her. She savored the taste of the sweetness of the peach against the salty flavor of his fingers.

Looking down at his feet, then back at her, he smiled sheepishly. "As a kid, I wanted to drive a garbage truck."

Her jaw dropped. Closed. Then opened again as she said, "Am I missing something in translation? You wished to drive a truck that picks up trash?"

"I did. When my parents argued, I would go outside to hide from the noise. Sometimes it got so loud I had to leave. So I rode my bike to follow the garbage truck. I would watch how that crusher took everyone's trash and crushed it down to almost nothing. As a kid that sounded very appealing."

Thinking of him pedaling full-tilt down the roads as a child put an ache in her heart she couldn't deny. "I am sorry your parents hurt you that way."

"I just want you to understand I take marriage and our children's happiness seriously."

His brown eyes met hers. They were heated with a ferocity she hadn't seen before.

This offer of a life together was real to him. His offer was genuine, determined. And from a very driven man. She needed to make up her mind, and soon, or she could fast lose all objectivity around Gervais.

Ten

It had only been three days since he'd gotten home from the loss in St. Louis. He needed time to think of his next strategy. And not just for the Hurricanes. With Erika, too.

Which was exactly why he'd pulled on his running shorts and shirt. Laced up his shoes and hit the pavement, footsteps keeping him steady.

Focused.

Sweat curled off his upper lip, the taste of salt heavy in his mouth. The humid Louisiana twilight hummed with the songs of the summer bugs and birds.

This always set his mind right. The sound of foot to pavement. Inhale. Exhale. The feel of sweat on his back.

He'd been quite the runner growing up. Always could

best his brothers in distance and speed. Especially Jean-Pierre, his youngest brother.

Jean-Pierre had to work harder than all his older brothers to keep up with them as they ran. Running had been something of a Reynaud rite of passage. Or so Gervais had made it out to be. He'd always pushed his brothers for a run. It was an escape from the yelling and fighting that went on at their home. Whether the family was at the ranch in Texas, on the expansive property on Lake Pontchartrain or on the other side of the globe, there was always room to run, and Gervais had made use of those secured lands to give them all some breathing space from the parental drama.

Slowing his pace, he stopped to tighten his shoelace. Looking at the sparkling water of the lake, he realized it had been too long since he talked to Jean-Pierre. Months.

Gervais knew he needed to call him…but things hadn't been the same since Jean-Pierre left Louisiana Tech to play for the Gladiators in New York. Sure, Jean-Pierre maintained a presence on the family compound, sharing upkeep of one of the homes where he stayed when he flew into town. But how often had that been over the past few years? Even in the off-season, Jean-Pierre tended to stick close to New York and his teammates on the Gladiators. When he did show up in New Orleans, it was to take his offensive line out on his boat or for a raucous party that was more for friends than family.

How Jean-Pierre managed to stay away from this quirky, lively city was beyond Gervais. When they were younger, the family had spent a lot of time in Texas. Which, make no mistake, Gervais loved, but there was a charm to New Orleans, a quality that left the place rarified.

He wanted to share those things with Erika. The cultural scene was unbeatable, and the food. Well, he'd yet to take her to his favorite dessert and dancing place. He pictured taking her out for another night on the Big Easy with him. She'd love it if she'd give him a chance to show her.

And though they'd fallen into a pattern over the past few days, he felt as distant as ever and all because she wouldn't commit even though they had children on the way. Sure, they made love nightly now. And he relished the way her body writhed beneath his touch. But it wasn't enough. He bit his tongue about the future and she didn't say anything about leaving.

Or staying.

And he wanted her to stay. Starting to run again, he picked up the intensity. Ran harder, faster.

He didn't want her to leave. He didn't want a repeat of London. Before he'd even woken up, she'd packed her things and let herself out of the hotel suite. Though it had been only one weekend, he had fallen for her. Now they'd spent days together.

Rather blissful days. Mind wandering, he thought to the last night in St. Louis when they'd explored the rooftop garden that was attached to their hotel suite. There'd been a slight chill in the air, but things between them had been on fire. In his memory, he traced the curves on her body.

Though she might be pumping the brakes on the future, he was getting to know her. To see past her no-nonsense facade to the woman who was a little sarcastic, kindhearted and generous.

The thought of her just leaving again like in London… it made his gut sink.

Rounding the last corner on his run, he didn't hold back. He sprinted all out, as if that would allow him to hold on to Erika.

This was damn awful timing, too. He knew he needed to focus on his career. To turn the Hurricanes into a financial dynasty to back the championship team Dempsey assured them they had in place. And this thing with Erika—whatever it might be—was not helping him. Sure, he'd nabbed that sponsor in Chicago. But every day he spent with her was a day that he wasn't securing another sponsor that would make the Hurricanes invincible as a business and not just a team. They'd been teetering on the brink of folding when he'd purchased them, and he'd reinvigorated every facet since then, but his work was far from done to keep them in the black.

But damn. He could not. No. He *would* not just let her leave as she had before. This wasn't just about the fact they were having a family, or that they were amazing together in bed.

Quickening his pace, he saw the Reynaud compound come into sight. The light was on in Erika's bedroom.

His grandfather had taught him a few things when he was a kid. Two of the most important: *build your dream* and *family is everything.* Two simple statements. And he wanted Erika to be a part of that. To create the kind of home that his own kids would never want to run from.

Sitting cross-legged on a cushioned chair in the massive dining room, Erika absently spread raspberry jam on her puffy biscuit. Try as she might, she couldn't force her mind to be present. To be in the moment.

Instead, her thoughts drifted back to Gervais and last night. He'd knocked on her door after his run. She'd opened the door, let him in. And he'd showered her in determined, passion-filled kisses. There was an urgency, a sincerity in their lovemaking last night. A new dimension to sex she had never thought possible.

Last night had made it even harder for her to be objective about their situation. She wanted Gervais. But she also wanted what was best for them both. Balancing that need seemed almost impossible.

A motion in the corner of her eye brought her back to the present. She found Gervais's grandfather filling his plate at the buffet with pork grillades and grits, a buttered biscuit on the side.

Gracious, she could barely wait for the morning to wane so the queasy feeling would subside and she could indulge in more of the amazing food of this region. Everything tasted so good, or perhaps that was her pregnancy hormones on overload. Regardless, she was hungry but didn't dare try more for a couple more hours yet.

She looked back at Gervais's grandfather, keeping her eyes off the plate of food. Leon hadn't gone with them to St. Louis, but Gervais had explained how travel anywhere other than from his homes in New Orleans and Texas left the old man disoriented.

He took his place at the head of the table, just to the left of her, and poured himself a cup of thick black coffee from the silver carafe. "So you're carrying my first great-grandchild—" He tapped his temple near his gray hair. "Grandchildren. You're having twins. I remember that. Some days my memory's not so good, but that's sticking in my brain and making me happy. A legacy. And if you won't find it disrespectful of me to say so, I believe it's going to be a brilliant, good-looking legacy." He toasted her with his china coffee cup.

"Thank you, sir. No disrespect taken at all. That's a delightful thing to say, especially the smart part." She gave him a wink as she picked at her biscuit. Praise of her intelligence was important. Erika had worked hard to be more than a pretty princess. Wanted her worth and merit to be attached to her mind's tenacity. To realize her dreams of setting up a nurse-practitioner practice of her own someday, one with an entire section devoted to homeopathic medicines and mood-leveling aromatherapy.

"That's important." He sipped more of his coffee before digging into his breakfast. "We have a large family empire to pass along, and I want it to go into good hands. I didn't do so well with my own children. But my grandkids, I'm damn proud of them."

"Gervais will make a good father." Of that she had no doubt. He was already so attentive.

"He works too much and takes on too much responsibility to prove he's not like his old man, but yes, he will take parenthood seriously. He may need some books, though. To study up, since he didn't have much of a role model. He sure knows what not to do, though." A laugh rasped from the man's cracked lips and he finished more of his coffee.

"I believe you played a strong part in bringing up your grandchildren." She reached for the carafe and offered to refill his cup, even though she wasn't drinking coffee. She stuck to juice and water these days.

He nodded at her, eyes turning inward as if he was reading something she couldn't see. "I tried to step in where I could. Didn't want to bring up spoiled, silver-spoon-entitled brats again." His focus returned to her. "I like that you went into the military. That speaks well of your parents."

Her mother and father had pitched an unholy fit over that decision, but she would not need to say as much. "It was an honor to serve my country."

"Good girl. What do you plan to do now that your studies are on hold?"

Technically, they weren't. She would be back in university in autumn.

"When I return to school, I will undertake the program to become a nurse-practitioner, even as a single mother." And she would. No matter how long it took.

"Really? I didn't expect you to, um—"

"Work for a living? Few do, even after my military service." Her voice went softer than she would have liked.

"You'll take good care of my grandson when I'm

gone?" His question pierced her tender heart on a morning when her emotions were already close to the surface.

"Sir, you appear quite spry to me."

"That's not what I mean and if you're wanting to be a nurse-practitioner, you probably know that." He tapped his temple again. "It's here that I worry about giving out too soon. The doctors aren't sure how fast. Sometimes I prefer the days I don't remember talking to those experts."

"I am so very sorry." She hadn't spent a lot of time with Leon Reynaud. But she could tell he was a good man who cared a lot about his family. And the stories Gervais told her only confirmed that.

"Thank you. Meanwhile, I want to get to know you and spend time with you so you can tell my great-grans all about me." He pointed with his biscuit for emphasis and she couldn't help but smile.

"That sounds delightful," she said to Gramps, but her eyes trailed over his head. To Gervais, who strode into the dining hall.

Sexy. That was the only word that pulsed in her mind as she looked at him. Dressed in a blue button-down shirt, he looked powerful.

"Don't mind me," he mumbled, smiling at her. "Just grabbing some breakfast before heading to the office. You can go back to telling embarrassing stories about me, Gramps."

Gramps chuckled. "I was just getting ready to tell my favorite."

Gervais gave him a faux-injured grin, swiping a muffin and apple from the table.

He stopped next to her. Gave her a hug and a kiss. Not a deep kiss or even lingering. Instead, he gave her one of those familiar kisses. A kiss that spoke of how they'd been together before. That they knew each other's bodies and taste well. She bit her bottom lip where the taste of him lingered, minty, like his toothpaste.

As he walked away, everything felt...right. Being with him seemed so natural, as if they had been doing this for years. It'd be so easy—too easy—to slide right into this life with him.

And that scared her clean through to her toes.

It had been a long day at the office, one of the longest since their return from St. Louis. Gervais had tried his best to secure a new technology sponsor for the Hurricanes, a west coast company with deep pockets that was currently expanding their presence in New Orleans. The fit was perfect, but the corporate red tape was nightmarish, and the CEO at the helm hadn't been as forward thinking as the CFO, whom Gervais had met on another deal the year before. Not everyone understood the tremendous advertising power of connecting with an NFL team, and the CEO of the tech company had been reluctant. Stubborn. It had been a hellish day, but at least the guy hadn't balked at the deal. Yet.

Gervais had left work midday to talk with some of Gramps's doctors. They were discussing treatment plans and some of the effects of his new medicines. All he wanted to do was give the best he could to his family.

Family. Gramps. Hurricanes. Jean-Pierre. Work and Reynaud business had swirled in his mind all day. The only thing he wanted to do this evening was see Erika. The thought of her, waiting at home for him, had kept him fighting all day. Besides, he had a gift for her and he couldn't wait to present it to her.

Walking into her room, he felt better just seeing her. She was sitting on the chaise longue, staring blankly at her suitcase.

Her unzipped suitcase.

That fleeting moment of good feeling vanished. Was she leaving? If he had come home later, would she have already been gone, just like London?

Taking a deep breath, he set aside his gift for her and surveyed the room. The two arrangements of hydrangeas and magnolias were on her dresser alongside an edible bouquet of fruit. He'd had them sent to her today while he was at work. For her to think about their time in St. Louis together.

As he continued to look around the room, he didn't see any clothes pulled out. So they were all either in the drawers or in her bag.

He hoped they were still in the drawers. Gervais didn't want her to go. Instead, he wanted her to stay here. With him. Be part of his family.

Tapping the suitcase, he stared at Erika "That's not full, is it?"

He tried to sound light. Casual. The opposite of his current mental state.

She looked up quickly, her eyes such a startling shade of blue. "No, of course not. Why would you think that?"

"You left once before without a word." He wanted to

take her in his arms and coax her into bed for the day, not think about her leaving.

"I promised you I would stay for two weeks and I meant it. After that, though, I have to make a decision."

He tensed.

"Why? Why the push?"

"I need to move forward with my life at some point." Chewing her lip, she gestured at the suitcase.

"I've asked you to marry me and move in with me, yet still you hold back. Let me help support you while you make a decision, with time if not money, wherever you are." He would do that for her and more.

She looked at him with a steady, level gaze. "Seriously? Haven't we had this discussion already? We have time to make these decisions."

"The sooner we plan, the sooner we can put things into place."

"Do not rush, damn it. That is not the way I am. My parents learned that when they tried to push me into their way of life, their plans for me." Her gaze was level, icy.

"So you plan to leave, just not now?"

"I do not know what I am planning." Her voice came out in a whisper, a slight crack, as well. "I am methodical. I need to think through all of the options and consequences."

"Is that what you did the morning you left me? Stayed up and thought about why we needed to turn our backs on the best sex ever?" Dropping onto the edge of the bed across from her, he caught her gaze. Looked at the intensity of her blue eyes. She was damn sexy.

Beautiful. And he wasn't going to let her walk away as if this was nothing.

"Best sex ever? I like the sound of that." She licked her lips seductively, leaned toward him, her breasts pressing against her glittery tank top.

So tempting. And definitely not the direction he needed to take with her.

He raised his brow at her. "You're trying to distract me with your beautiful body."

"And you are using flattery. We need more than that." Crossing her arms, she scrutinized his face.

"I've made it clear I understand that. That's what our time together has been about. But I am willing to use everything I have at my disposal. I am not giving up."

"Everything?" She gestured to the flowers, the candy and a small jewelry box.

He'd forgotten about the gift he'd brought for her.

Pushing off the bed, he approached her, leaned on the arms of the chaise longue. He kissed her forehead, one arm around her, the other still cradling the box. "Flattery, which is easy because you are so very lovely. Charming words are tougher for me because I am a businessman, but for you, I will work so very hard with the words. And, yes, with gifts, too. Will you at least open it?"

She took the box from his hands, eyes fixed on his. Her fingers found the small bow. Gently, she slowly pulled the white bow off. The Tiffany box was bare, undressed now.

Erika lifted the lid, let out a small gasp. Two heart earrings encrusted in diamonds glinted back at her.

Gervais's voice dropped half an octave. "It made me think of our children. Two beautiful hearts."

He tucked a knuckle under her chin and raised it to see her face. Tears welled in her eyes.

Pulse pounding, he put his arms around her, held her tight to his chest. "I didn't mean to make you cry."

She shook her head, her silky blond hair tickling his nose. "It is sweet, truly. Thoughtful. A wonderful gift."

Kneeling in front of her, he wiped the tears off her pale cheeks. He'd wanted to get her something meaningful. Drawing her hands in his, he kissed the back of each one, then the insides of her wrists in the way he knew sent her pulse leaping. He could feel it even now as he rubbed his thumbs against her silky skin. "I want this to work. Tell me what I can do to make that happen. It is yours."

Her eyes flooded with conflicting feelings. It was as if he could see into her thought process where she worked so hard to weigh the pros and cons of a future. Somehow he knew she was at the precipice of the answer she'd been looking for. One he was scared as hell to receive.

And, cursing himself for his weakness, he couldn't resist this one last chance to sway the outcome. To make her want to stay. So he kissed her deeply, ebbing away the pressure of speech to make room for the pleasure they both needed.

Eleven

Gervais had Erika in his arms and he wanted that to go on for... He couldn't think of a time he wouldn't want her. Every cell inside him ached to have her. So much so his senses homed in to her. Almost to the exclusion of all else. Almost to the point where he lost sight of the fact he'd left the door ajar.

And now someone was knocking lightly on that door.

With more than a little regret, he set her away from him and struggled to regulate his breathing before turning to the door to find...a security guard?

Hell. How could he have forgotten for even a second that his family's wealth and power carried risk? They needed to stay on watch at all times.

Security guard James Smithson stood on the other side of the half-open door, his chiseled face grave.

Gervais had always liked James—a young guy, athletic and focused. James had almost made the cut for the team. The poor kid was in an interesting position; he'd declined a college football scholarship when his high school girlfriend became pregnant. James attended an online school while helping raise their son, but he'd shown up at a couple of Hurricanes training camps with impressive drive, even though his stats weren't quite strong enough.

So before Dempsey could send him home, Gervais had taken him aside and found out he had skills off the field, too. He'd offered him help forming his own security company, making him a part of the Hurricanes family.

"Sorry to disturb you, sir, but we have some unexpected company."

"I don't accept unexpected guests. You know that." Gervais stared at the guard. Who, to be fair, was doing a damn good job at not looking at Erika in her tight-fitting sparkly tank top that revealed her killer curves. Even so, he found himself wanting to wrap her up in a sheet. Just to be safe.

"I understand that, sir," James assured him. "But…"

Erika looked back and forth between the guard and Gervais. "I'll leave the two of you to talk." She closed the jewelry box and clutched it to her chest. "If you'll excuse me."

James held up a hand. "Ma'am, I believe you'll want to stay."

Ericka's face twisted in confusion. "I'm not sure how I can be of help—"

James scrubbed his jaw awkwardly. "It's your family. Their limos are just now coming through the front gate."

Gervais blinked slowly. "Limos?" Plural?

"My family?" Erika stammered, color draining from her skin. "*All* of my family?"

James gave a swift nod, his gun just visible in a shoulder harness under his sports jacket. "It appears so, ma'am. Both of your parents, four sisters, three of them married and some children, I believe?"

Gervais scratched the back of his head right about where an ache began. Talk about a baptism of fire meeting all the in-laws at once. So many. "I think we're going to need to air out the guesthouse."

The pressure of a headache billowed between Erika's temples. As she stood in the grand living room, attention drawn outside, past the confines of this room, she felt everything hit her at once. First, her conflicting feelings for Gervais, and now this.

Her entire family, down to her nieces, was here. Now. Her eyes trailed past the bay windows to where Gervais, her father, Gervais's brothers and his grandfather stood on the patio. Having drinks as if this was the most casual affair ever. As if this was something they had done together for years. Gervais had a gift with that, taking charge of a situation and putting everyone at ease.

She'd spent so much time focusing on the reasons to hold back, she forgot to look for the reasons they should. There was a lot to admire about this man. His obvious love of his family. His honorability in his standing up to care for his children. And the way he handled his business affairs with a mix of savvy and compassion. Her heart was softening toward him daily, and her resolve was all but gone.

And of course there was the passionate, thorough way he made love to her. A delicious memory tingled through her. She tore her eyes from him before she lost the ability to think reasonably at all.

Her father, Bjorn Mitras, slapped his knee enthusiastically at something Gervais had said. So they were getting along.

The mood inside the living room was decidedly less jovial. She could feel her sisters and mother sizing her up. Determining what Erika ought to do. And if she had to bet, getting her Master's in Nursing wasn't even on the table anymore. They'd never supported her ambitions. And if she was carrying a male child...well, they'd certainly have a lot of opinions to throw at her.

For the first time since learning she was pregnant, Erika felt alone.

She had hoped for an ally in Fiona, but Fiona hadn't come to meet everyone. She wasn't feeling well. Erika was not feeling all that great herself right now. Her family overwhelmed her in force.

Turning reluctantly from the bay windows, she studied her mother. Arnora Mitras had always been a slight, slim woman. Unlike other royals, she recycled outfits. But Arnora was a friend of many fashion designers. She was always draped in finery, things quite literally off the runway.

Her four sisters—Liv, Astrid, Helga and Hilda—stood in the far corner, discussing things in hushed tones. The twins, Helga and Hilda, both had the same nervous tic, tracing the outline of their bracelets. It was something that they had both done since they were little girls. Erika squinted at them, trying to figure out what had them on edge.

But it was Astrid who caught her gaze. Blue eyes of equal intensity shone back at her. Astrid gave a curt nod, her honey-blond bob falling into her face.

It was a brief moment of recognition, but then Astrid turned back to the conversation. Back to whispering.

Three of her sisters had married into comfort, but not luxury. Not like what the Reynauds offered. And they lived across Europe, leading quieter lives. No male heirs, no extravagance. A part of Erika envied that anonymity, especially now.

Of course, Gervais had seen to every detail. And in record time. He called in all the staff and security. Arranged what looked like a small state dinner in record time. He even had nannies brought in for her nieces.

Beignets, fruit and pralines were decadently arranged into shapes and designed. It looked almost too beautiful to eat. Erika watched as her sisters loaded their plates with the pastries and fruit, but they eyed the pralines with distrust. They weren't an open-minded bunch. They preferred to stick to what they knew. Which was also probably why they skipped over the iced tea and went straight for the coffee. That was familiar.

"Mother—" the word tumbled out of Erika's mouth "—some advance notice of your visit would have been nice."

"And give you the opportunity to make excuses to put us off? I think not."

Sighing unabashedly, Erika trudged on. "I was not putting you off, Mother. I was simply…"

"Avoiding us all," Helga finished for her as she approached. The rest of the Mitras women a step behind her.

"Hardly. I wanted time to prepare for your visit and to ensure that every detail was properly attended to."

Helga gave a wave to the spread of food and raised her brow. She clearly didn't believe Erika's protest. "This place is amazing. You landed well, sister."

"I am only visiting and getting things in order for our babies' sake." Erika's words were clipped, her emotions much more of a tangle.

"Well, you most certainly have something in common. Relationships have been built on less. I say go for it. Chase that man down until he proposes." The last word felt like nails on a chalkboard in Erika's ears. She schooled her features neutral, just as she had done when she was a translator. No emotions walked across her face.

Erika stayed diplomatically quiet.

Her mother's delicately arched eyebrow lifted, and she set her bone china coffee cup down with a slow and careful air. "He has already proposed? You two are getting married?"

"No, I did not say we are getting married."

"But he *has* proposed," Hilda pressed gently.

"Stop. This is why I would have preferred you wait to meet him. Give Gervais and me a chance to work out the details of our lives without family interference, and then we will share our plan."

Liv waggled her fingers toward the French doors leading to the vast patio. "*His* family is here."

"And they are not pushy," Erika retorted with conviction. She wasn't backing down from this. Not a chance.

"We are not pushy, either. We just want what is best for you." Hilda's porcelain complexion turned ruddy, eyes widening with hurt and frustration like during their childhood whenever people laughed at her lisp. She always had been the most sensitive of the lot.

Smoothing her green dress, Liv—always the prettiest, and the most rebellious, the infamous sex tape being the least of her escapades—took a deep breath and touched her hair. "I think all of this travel has made me a bit weary. I shall rest and we will talk later."

And with that her mother, Liv, Helga and Hilda all left the grand living room, heels clacking against the ground.

But Astrid didn't leave. She hung back, eyes fixed on Erika.

Anger burned in Erika's belly. Astrid was her oldest sister. The one who always told her what to do. She had been the sister to lecture her as a child. Erika fully anticipated some version of that pseudo-parental "advice" to spill out of Astrid's lips.

"Keep standing up for yourself. You are doing the right thing."

Gaping, Erika steadied herself on the back of the tapestry sofa. "Seriously? I appreciate the support but

I have to say it would be nice to have with Mother present."

Astrid shrugged. "She is frightening and strong willed. We all know that. But you do understand, you are strong, too. That is why we pushed you off the balcony first."

"Wow, thanks," Erika grumbled, recalling the terrifying drop from balcony to homemade trampoline.

"You are welcome." Astrid closed her in a tight embrace. In a half whisper, she added, "I love you, sister."

"I love you, too." That much of life was simple.

If only the other relationships—her relationship with Gervais—could be as easily understood. Or maybe they could. Perhaps the time had come to stop fighting her emotions and to embrace them.

Starting with embracing Gervais.

With the arrival of Erika's family, work for the Hurricanes had taken a backseat. Not that he would have had it any other way. They were his children's aunts and grandparents. They were important to him. He had to win them over—particularly her father, the king, not that King Bjorn had shown any sign of disapproval.

But important or not, they were the reason he was just now getting to his charts and proposals in the wee small hours of the morning.

Gervais pressed Play on the remote. He was holed up in the mini theater. He had a few hours of preseason games from around the league to catch up on. This was where he'd been slacking the most. Hadn't spent much time previewing the talent on the other teams yet. Because while Dempsey would fine-tune a solid fifty-three-man roster from the talent currently working out with the team, Gervais needed to cultivate a backup plan for injuries and for talent that didn't pan out. That meant he needed to familiarize himself with what else was out there, which underrated players might need a new home with the Hurricanes before the October trade deadline.

A creak from the door behind him caused him to turn around in his seat. Erika was there, in the doorway. A bag of popcorn in one hand, with two sodas in the other.

She certainly was a sight for his tired eyes. He drank her in appreciatively, noting the way her bright pink sundress fit her curves, the gauzy fabric swishing when she walked. The halter neck was the sort of thing he could untie with a flick of fabric, and he was seized with the urge to do just that.

As soon as possible. Damn.

"I thought this could be like a date." She gave him a sly smile, bringing her magnolia scent with her as she neared him, a lock of blond hair grazing his arm.

He took the sodas from her and set them in the cup holders on either side of the leather chairs in the media room.

"Well, then, best date ever."

"That seems untrue." Worry and exhaustion lined her voice. "I am sorry about my family arriving unexpectedly. And for how much time they are taking out of your workday."

"It's no trouble at all. They are my children's grandparents. That's huge." Pausing the game, he gave her a genuine smile, conceding that he wouldn't be giving the footage his full attention now. But he had notes on the talent across the league, of course. As an owner, he didn't run the team alone.

And right now nothing was more important to him than Erika and his children.

Settling deeper into the chair beside him, Erika flipped her long hair in front of one shoulder and centered the bag of popcorn between them.

"I also appreciate how patient you have been. And my sisters loved the tours through New Orleans." Erika leaned on his shoulder, the scent of her shampoo flooding his mind with memories of London. St. Louis. And last night. Making love, their bodies and scents and need mingling, taking them both to a higher level of satisfaction than he'd ever experienced.

Damn. He loved that. Loved that this smell made her present in his mind.

"Of course." He breathed, kissed her head, inhaled the scent of her hair and thought of their shower together.

Her breath puffed a little faster from her mouth. She nibbled her bottom lip and gestured to the screen. "May I ask what you are doing?"

Gervais hit Play, a game springing to life. "Well, I have to get a feel for who is out there. I have a team to build. So I may have to replace my current rookies with some of these guys."

Erika nodded. "And why is this so important to you? Why do you spend so much time on football when, according to the press, they are worth only a fraction of your overall portfolio?"

"Someone's been doing her research," he noted. Impressed.

"I was not joking when I told you that I am trying to figure out where to go from here. I am thinking through all possible paths." Her blue gaze locked on him. "Including the one you have proposed."

His chest ached with the need to convince her that was the best. But he restrained himself. Focused on her question.

"Why the focus on football?" he repeated, reaching into the popcorn bag for a piece to feed her. "My family is a lot like yours. They come with expectations. But I have my own expectations, and I've always wanted to carve out something that was all mine within the vast Reynaud holdings. Some success that I made myself, that was not handed to me. Does that make any sense?"

He presented her with the popcorn and she opened her lips. His touch lingered a bit longer than necessary against her soft mouth.

She chewed before she answered. "You want to stand on your own two legs?"

Gervais smiled inwardly. Her idiom use was so close. "Something like that. If I can stand on my own two feet, make this team into something..." His mind searched for the correct words.

"Then no one can take that away from you. It is yours alone."

Gervais nodded, stroking her arm. "Exactly. I imagine that's why you want your Master's in Nursing so badly. So that is holistically yours."

"Mmm," she said, tracing light lines on his chest.

"Very wise of you. You have been listening to me, I see."

Her touch stirred him. Heat rushed through his veins as he set aside the remote.

"We are more alike than you think." He curled an arm around her shoulders and drew her closer, his fingers skimming through her silky hair to the impossibly soft skin of her upper arm.

"Because we are both stubborn and independent?" She slid her finger into the knot of his tie and loosened the material.

"It's more than that." He wrenched the tie off, consigning the expensive Italian silk to the floor.

"We are both struggling to meet the expectations of too much helpful family?" She arched a pale brow at him, all the while fingering open buttons on his shirt.

The hell with waiting.

He slid an arm under her knees and lifted her up and onto his lap, straddling him. Her long sundress spilled over her thighs, covering her while exposing just the smallest hint of satin panties where she sat on his thighs.

"And we both need to lose ourselves in each other right now." His fingers sifted through her hair, seeking the ribbon that secured the halter top of her sundress.

"You are correct," she assured him, edging down his thighs so that their hips met.

Her breasts flattened to his chest.

A hungry groan tore from his throat.

He kissed her hard, his control fractured after so many days of thinking through every move with her, of strategizing this relationship like the most important deal of his life. Because while it was all that and more, Erika was also the hottest, most incredible woman he'd ever met, and he wanted her so badly he ached.

She met each hungry swipe of his tongue with soft sighs and teasing moans that threatened to send him right over the edge. Already, her fingers worked the fastening of his belt, her thighs squeezing his hips.

"This day has been too much," she admitted, her whispered confession one of the few times she'd confided her feelings. "I need you. This."

And he wanted to give it to her. Now and forever.

But he knew better than to rattle her with talk of forever. Understood she was still coming to terms with a future together. So he forced himself to be everything she needed right now.

Flicking free the tie at her neck, he edged away from the kiss just enough to admire the fall of the gauzy top away from her beautiful breasts. Her skin was so pale she almost glowed in the darkened theater, his tanned hands a dark shadow against her as he cupped the full weight of one breast.

Molding her to his palm, he teased his thumb across the pebbled tip, liking the way her hips thrust harder against his as he did. She was more sensitive than ever, the least little touch making her breath come faster. Making her release quicker.

Just thinking about that forced him to move faster, one hand skimming down her calf to slip beneath the hem of her long dress. He stroked her bare knee. Smoothed up her slender thigh. Skimmed the satin of panties already damp for him.

She cried out his name as he worked her through the thin fabric, coaxing an orgasm from her with just a few strokes. Her back arched as the tension pulsed through her in waves, her knees hugging him until the spasms slowed.

He didn't waste time searching out a condom, since they no longer needed one. He let her go just long enough to shove aside the placket of his pants and free his erection.

She took over then, her fingers curling the hard length and stroking up to the tip until his heart damn near beat its way out of his chest. He kissed her deeply, distracting her from her erotic mission, leaving him free to enter her.

And oh, damn.

The slick heat of her squeezed him, the scent of her skin and taste of her lips like a drug for his senses. He gripped her hips, guiding her where he wanted. Where he needed. And looking up at her in the half-light reflected from the dim screen, he could see that she was as lost as him. Her plump lips were moist and open, her eyes closed as she rode him, finding her pleasure with as much focus and intensity as him.

He must have said her name, because her eyes opened then. Her blue gaze locked on his.

And that did it.

More than any touch. Any kiss. Any sexy maneuver in the dark. Just having Erika right there with him drove him over the edge. The pleasure flared over his skin and up his spine, rocking him. He held on tight to her, surprised to realize she had found her own peak again right along with him, their bodies in perfect sync.

After the waves of pleasure began to fade and the sweat on their bodies cooled, he stroked her spine through that long veil of her hair, savoring the feel of her in his arms, her warm weight so welcome in his lap. He wanted her every night. Wanted to be the one to take care of her and ease her. Pleasure her.

But even as his feelings surged, he could tell she was pulling back. Throwing up a seemingly impenetrable wall of ice as she edged back and tugged her dress into place. Her family's arrival had shaken her. Awakened an instinct to define herself in opposition to their expectations.

A part of him understood that. And was damn proud of her, too. But that same urge that motivated her to stand her ground, meet her parents and family dead-on, might also be the reason he felt frozen out.

The more he thought about it, the more real seemed the idea of losing not just his children, but her, too.

And as if she sensed his thoughts, she got to her feet. "Gervais, my family's here, so I would appreciate it if we didn't sleep together with them nearby."

"Seriously?" He propped himself up on his elbows.

"I know it may seem silly with the babies on the way, but…them being here? I need space."

He studied her face, her platinum-blond hair tumbling around her shoulders. "Damn it, Erika, all I've done is honor your need for space, taking cues off you."

"A few short days. Less than a month. And you call that space? Time?" Her throat moved. "Clearly we have very different ideas about taking our time. Maybe we don't understand each other nearly as well as you think."

Frustration fired inside him as he felt victory slip away word by word. He tugged on his pants, all the while searching for the right words and coming up short.

Not that it mattered, since before he could speak, she'd left the room. The click of that door made it clear.

She was running scared and he wasn't welcome to join her now.

If ever.

Twelve

The excitement of the fans at the home Hurricanes game was dwarfed in comparison to the buzz going on in the owners' box.

Erika sat against the leather chair, taking it all in, her heart in her throat after the way she'd left things with Gervais last night. But the way he made her feel scared her down to her toes. He made her want too much at a time when she had to be more careful than ever about protecting her heart and her future.

Gramps Leon called out to the Mitras clan. "Did Erika tell you how the Reynauds came into their fortune?"

"No, Leon, she hasn't shared much of anything with us. We'd love to know. American origin stories are so fascinating," Hilda said darkly, shooting her a daggered look across the spread of shrimp gumbo and decadent brownies. Erika rolled her eyes, moving closer to the glass to get a look at the field. Somehow, this game she had disliked so much was starting to make sense to her.

"Grampa Leon, we all know that story," Fiona said with a light laugh, her hands wringing together. She was nervous but Erika couldn't tell why.

"Yes, but the beautiful princesses and queen haven't. And they want to. Who am I to deny them that?" he said with a wink at Hilda, whose face was already turning into a toothy grin.

"It was a high-stakes poker game. My surly old Cajun ancestor was sweating as he stared at his hand of cards. The stakes were incredibly high, you see," Gramps Leon began, leaning on his knees.

"What were the stakes, Leon?" Queen Arnora asked, on her best behavior, since Erika had been emphatic with her mother that histrionics would not be tolerated. The babies were Erika and Gervais's, not potential little royal pawns.

Arnora had vowed she simply wanted to bond with their expanding family and was thrilled over impending grandparenthood.

"If my riverboat grandpa won, he would get a ship out of the deal. But if he lost, he would have to sign a non-compete. And stay working for the tyrant captain who kept him away from home for months on end. Needless to say, the cards laid out right for him and he won the first ship in the fleet. The Reynaud family empire was born. Just like that." He snapped his fingers, eyes alight with a new audience to entertain. "The rest is history. The family has been successful ever since. Especially my grandboys."

King Bjorn inclined his head. "You feel responsible for your grandchildren's success?"

"Yessir, King Bjorn. I'm proud of all of those boys. Feel like I practically raised them myself. Though I kind of did," Gramps Leon wheezed, eyes drifting to Theo, who shrank in the back corner, "My son almost made it big…eh. No matter. My grandboys did. That's what matters in the end."

Erika watched as Theo fidgeted with his drink, balling up a cocktail napkin in his right fist. She knew he hadn't been the best father, but a small part of her felt sympathy for him.

"And what did all your grandchildren do?" Arnora asked lightly, swirling the champagne in her glass.

Erika had often wondered how her mother had such ease with others but not as much with her children. Her mom took her role as a royal, a liaison to the world, seriously. Erika looked around at the Reynaud family and saw their bond, but not only that. She saw their relaxed air. The way they kept life…real. Connected. She wanted that for her children, as well.

And yet she'd pushed her babies' father away the night before out of fear of living like her parents.

Gramps Leon's dark eyes gleamed with pride and affection. "Well, you know Gervais bought his own team. I figure they'll make it big soon the way that boy works. And Dempsey is the youngest coach in the league's history. Henri is already a franchise quarterback looking for his first championship ring. Even Jean-Pierre is doing good things as a quarterback for that northern Yankee team. Where is he again?"

Theo cleared his throat. "New York. Jean-Pierre is the starting quarterback for the New York Gladiators." Pride pierced his words, and he lifted his eyes to meet Leon's. So he did care, Erika thought. It was just masked.

She wished it was that easy to tell what was going on with Gervais. Nothing he'd said so far betrayed any level of an emotional depth. Just sex. But that wasn't enough for her. And that was the reason she hadn't been able to help but pull away the night before.

Last night when she'd gone to him, she'd believed he might really care for her. Sure, the sex was great and he wanted to provide for their children. But she'd started to think that he also genuinely liked her, sex and children aside.

Before then, she'd been so sure of him. Of the decision she was close to making.

As she sat in the owners' box again, she realized she couldn't stop replaying seeing the bed empty when she woke up, knowing it was her fault for pushing him away but not knowing what she could have done differently. Erika would have continued to analyze the situation if it wasn't for the approach of Liv, her sister. The one that had been through the sex tape fiasco.

The scandal had almost cost Liv everything.

Liv narrowed her gunmetal eyes at Erika, pinning her. She sat next to Erika, hands firmly grasping the wineglass's stem. The smell of alcohol assaulted Erika's sense of smell, turning her stomach sour.

"Sister," she said lazily, "this family…"

Erika straightened, finishing the sentence for her. "Is filled with wonderful, loving people."

Liv nodded solemnly. "Yes. And how do you say— American royalty?"

Erika's eyes remained out toward the field, toward where Gervais stood with a reporter giving an interview, players and photographers around them. She would not be dignifying her sister's comment with a response.

"All I am trying to say, dear sister, is that you need to be here. You could be royalty for real if you did." Liv's words, spoken in a hushed tone, had a bit of a slur to them.

"That's not what matters to me. What matters is—" But the words caught in her throat as she watched Gervais get hit by two men locked in a tackle. Gervais was on the sidelines, knocked to his feet, his bare skull slamming back into the ground. Hard. Tackled on the sidelines with no equipment.

She barely registered what the Mitrases or the Reynauds were doing. In an instant, the panic that stayed her breath and speech was replaced by a need to move. A need for action. The damn need to get to his side.

Pushing her way to the door that led down to the stands, she ran smack into James, the security guard who had first alerted them that the whole Mitras clan was arriving. He stood at the door to the tunnels leading through the bowels of the stadium and out onto the field. His credentials were clipped to his jacket, a communication piece in his ear. "Princess, I am afraid I can't allow you onto the field. Please wait here. I promise to keep you updated about Mr. Reynaud."

James put a hand on her shoulder. Consoling? Or to restrain? Either way, it didn't matter to her because this man kept her from Gervais.

Years of practice drills during her time in the military pressed her muscles into action. Without sparing a second thought, she grabbed his hand and bent back his pinkie. A minor move but one that could quickly drive a man to his knees if she pushed farther. "James, I am a nurse, but I am also former military. I can flip you onto your back in a heartbeat and you cannot—will not—fight me because I am pregnant. Now, we can do this simply or we can make this difficult, but one way or another, I am going to Gervais."

James's eyes narrowed, then he exhaled through gritted teeth. "I could lose my job for this." He shook his head, rolling his eyes. "But come with me. You'll need my credentials to get through to the field."

She bit her lip hard in relief. "Thank you."

"Um, ma'am, could you let go of my pinkie?"

"Oh." She blinked fast, having forgotten she'd even still held him pinned. She released his hand and stepped back.

Wincing, he shook his hand. "Follow me."

She followed him through the corridors, urging him to go faster and barely allowing herself to breathe until she saw Gervais with her own eyes. He waved off his personal security team as soon as she came into sight, his face twisted in pain as the team doctor shone a small flashlight in front of his eyes, checking his pupils.

Her medical training came to the fore and took in his pale face. He sat on the ground, upright, and was not swaying. His respiration was even, steady. Reassuring signs. Her heart slowed from a gallop. He would need a more thorough exam, certainly, but at least he was conscious. Cognizant.

"Gervais? Are you okay?" Erika knelt beside him, then turned to the team's doctor, her voice calm and collected now. "Is he all right?"

On the field beside him, the game continued, the fans cheering over a play while Erika's focus remained on Gervais and all that mattered to her.

"I'm fine," Gervais growled, then winced, pressing his hand to the back of his head.

The doctor tucked away his flashlight into his bag. "He's injured, no question, given the size of that goose egg coming up. Probably a concussion. He should go to the emergency room to be checked over."

"Then let us go." She barked the command at the doctor. Meanwhile, the game had resumed playing, and she trailed behind him.

As she stepped out of the arena with Gervais, leaving her family behind, reality crashed into her. Her heart was in her throat for this man. He was the father of her children. But she barely knew him and already he'd turned her world upside down. She felt as if she, too, had taken a blow to the head and her judgment was scrambled. How could she care so much so soon?

What was she doing here? She had started to love him, but maybe she just loved the surface image. Maybe she'd done what her family had done—just looked at the surface. After all, he'd offered no feelings, no emotions to her. Just convenient arrangements for their children and sex. His marriage proposal had never included mention of love.

And she couldn't settle for less than everything from him, just as she wanted to give him her all.

What if in spite of all logic, she had fallen in love with him and he could never offer her his full heart?

There were only a few times in his life that Gervais had felt extreme elation and intense concern all at the same time. This was certainly being added to that tally.

Later that night as he stretched out in his own bed, Erika hovering, he was still replaying that moment Erika had rushed out to him. His head throbbed but his memories were crystal clear.

Watching Erika care enough about him to rush to his side filled him with a renewed purpose. He'd been blown away and more than a little unnerved watching her rush to his side, somehow having persuaded James to let her through security and out onto the field.

Make no mistake, he always wanted her there. By his side. But he didn't want any harm to come to her or their children, either. The thought of harm befalling her or their children by her own rash actions gnawed at him. The security was there for a reason. God, she was everything to him. Everything. And he wasn't sure how he could have missed out on realizing the depth of that.

They could be so good together, but it also seemed as if the risk of her pulling back was at an all-time high. All of her interactions with him since the CT scan came back had been rigid. Formalized. As if she was a nurse doing a job, not a woman tending to her lover.

That reaction clapped him upside the head harder than the wall of a football player that had crashed into him. Her reactions didn't add up. She had been so upset on the sidelines, so freaked out about what was happening to him. And now she was answering in snippets of sentences. He didn't want to upset her more, or keep her awake all night. But his family had been in and out of the room for hours. It was nearing morning before he finally had a moment alone with her.

His head throbbed far more from this situation than his minor concussion.

Propped up on the bed, he quietly said, "How did you get James to let you join me on the field?"

She flushed the most lovely shade of pink, her hand fidgeting with her blond hair draped over her shoulder. "I used some of my military skills to persuade him. Nothing extreme, given my condition, of course, just a small but painful maneuver."

"Seriously? Apparently, I need to have you train my security."

"And give away my secrets?" She gave him a princess-like annoyed scoff. "I think not. Besides, he should not have tried to keep me from you."

"While I find that sexy on one level, you have to be careful and think about the babies. What if you had been hurt?"

She shrugged, looking him square in the eye. "I was careful. You are the injured one. Now, relax. You may not be stressed but you have to stay awake. Do as the doctor instructed or I am taking you back to the hospital."

He felt the prickles of her emotions. Had to change the direction. Bring it back to breezy. Shooting her a sly smile, he said, "We could have sex. That would keep me awake."

"You're supposed to rest." Eyes narrowing with annoyance, Erika crossed her arms.

"Then take advantage of me. I'll just lie back and be very still." He closed his eyes, then half opened one of them to look at her. Hoping to elicit some sort of response out of her. Hoping to see that radiant smile spread across her face. Damn. He loved that smile.

"Oh, you think you are funny. But I am not laughing right now. You are injured and I am here to make sure you take care of yourself."

"You could tie me up so I don't get too...boisterous."

"Boisterous? Now, that's an interesting word choice and a challenge. But sadly, for your own health, I will have to hold strong against your boisterous charms. Let us play cards." There was no jest in her voice.

"Cards? Strip poker, maybe."

"No, thank you."

"Then I'll pass on the cards. I gotta confess, my vision is a little blurry." He held up his hand, trying to focus on his fingers. A dull ache pulled at him.

Turning, practically out the door to the room, Erika said, "I should get the doctor."

"The doctor has checked me. I've had an X-ray and MRI and CT scan. I'm fine. Concussed, but nothing the players don't face all the time. I'm not going to be a wimp in front of my team."

"They wear helmets."

"I have a thick head. Just ask anyone I work with. Or those I don't work with." He tried his best to crack that smile wide-open, but Erika's face was as solemn as ever. She was shutting him out and he didn't understand why.

"I'm not laughing."

"You want to be serious? Then let's be serious. Erika, I want you to move in with me. Hell, to be honest, I want you to marry me, but I will settle for you moving in here. Go to school here. Let's be together. Life is complicated enough. Let's enjoy more popcorn dates and sex in the screen room and every other room in this place. And in my cars. I have many, you know." The declaration was earnest. He wanted her. For now. Forever. And not just because they were having children together.

Erika slammed her hand on the desk, a quiet rage burning in her fine, regal features. "I am still not laughing, Gervais. We cannot build a relationship on sex. I need something meaningful. I have fought so hard to build a life for myself, to be seen as someone more than ornamental. A royal jewel in the crown meant to bear an heir to the line, defunct or not."

"Erika. It's not like that. I don't think of you as a crown jewel." Gervais searched her face, trying to understand her.

"All you have done since I told you I was pregnant is press for marriage. I have worked hard to gain my independence, my happiness, and I will fight for my children, as well. They deserve something more."

"Erika, I—" Gervais, the man who always had a plan, stammered, fighting for words.

Tears glistened in her eyes, but she stood tall, her shoulders braced as she backed away. "I will wake one of your brothers. It is morning anyway." Erika turned, was already to the threshold and then gone before he could even think of words to delay her.

He had botched this chance to win her over. And what a helluva time to realize just how much he loved her, this proud, strong woman. He loved her intelligence, her passion, even her stubbornness. He adored every hair on her head.

He loved her so deeply he knew any fear of repeating his father's mistakes would not happen. Gervais loved Erika. Real love. The kind that he knew damn well was rare in this world.

And in rushing her, he may have ruined his chance to have her.

As Erika let her feet dangle over the edge of the dock, she focused her attention out on the lake's waters. The late-afternoon sun cast golden shimmers on the surface of the water.

She felt as if the whole day had been a training exercise. Nothing had felt real to her. Since she stormed out of Gervais's room last night, Erika had felt disoriented.

The problem was simple. Despite logic and reason, she was madly in love with Gervais. These past few days had proved how easy it would be to fall into a routine together.

But they had also shown her how difficult it would be for them to become more than…well, whatever this was.

A breeze stirred her loose blond hair, pushing strands in front of her eyes. Though it was humid, and the bugs played a loud symphony, she was comforted by the noises, smells and sights of this foreign land. It was starting to feel a bit like home. Another confusing feeling to muddle through.

The wind gusted stronger, stirring the marsh grass into a beautiful shudder. Boats zipped a ways off from the dock, and she watched the wakes crest and crash into each other.

It was practically silent, except for the boats and bugs. Everyone had gone. She'd packed her family into their limos, watched from the dock until the landscape of New Orleans swallowed them up.

The Reynauds were gone on a day trip. Theo's idea, actually. He'd even taken Gramps with them. All the Reynaud men, save for Jean-Pierre, on one trip in one spot. Probably something that didn't happen too often.

Inching backward on the dock, she pulled her knees to her chest. Erika was at a complete loss of what to do.

If only it could be as simple as the word *love*. She loved her children. She loved their father. But she still didn't know if he loved her back. On the one hand they hadn't known each other long, yet she was certain of her feelings. She needed him to be just as sure.

Her head spun with it all.

And her heart twisted.

She knew what she wanted, but it didn't make sense. She wanted to say to hell with logic and stay here with Gervais. To move in. To love him. To build their family together and pray it would all work out.

Footsteps echoed along the dock, startling her an instant before she heard Gervais's deep voice.

"You did not leave with your family."

Whipping her head up, she took him in. Fully. And a lump formed in the back of her throat.

"Did you think that I would do that without saying goodbye to you?" She would never have done something so cruel. Not after what she felt for him and all they'd been through together.

His chin tipped, the moonlight beaming around him. "Is this your farewell, then?"

"I am not going home with them."

He pressed further, drawing near to her. "And to school in the UK?"

Decision upon decision. Layer upon layer. "Do you think I should?"

"I want you to stay here but I cannot make this decision for you. I don't want to rush you."

His answer surprised her. "I expected you to try to persuade me."

"I've made my wishes clear. I want you to stay. I want us to build a life. But I can see you're afraid. I'll wait as long as you need." He knelt to her level, touched her face with his steady hand.

She bristled. "I am not afraid. I am wary. There is a difference."

"Is there?"

She churned over his words. "If you want to mince words in translation, then all right. I am afraid of making the wrong choice and having our children suffer because of it."

"And you think we are the wrong choice?"

"I think that I love you." There. It was out there. This was how she'd make her decision. Let him know exactly where she stood.

"I know that I love you."

She swallowed hard and blinked back tears, barely daring to believe what she was hearing. "You do?"

"I absolutely do. No question in my mind." His voice wrapped around her heart like a blanket, soothing and private and intimate all at once. He was…everything.

"I believe you and I want so very much to believe that will be enough."

"Then be willing to challenge that warrior spirit of yours and fight for what we feel for each other."

Fight? Erika had been used to fighting for the things that mattered to her. Maybe this battleground wasn't so foreign, after all. "Fight."

"Yes, stay here. Get to know me. Let me get to know you. And every day for the rest of our lives we'll get to know more and more about each other. That's how it works."

"I will move in with you?" The idea was tantalizing this time and she wondered why she had dismissed it so readily before. Out of pride? The thought of losing herself in her family again reminded her how hard she had fought for her freedom to live her life. And truth be told, she wanted to live here, in this fascinating town with this even more fascinating man. She wanted to give her children a family life like the Reynauds.

She wanted Gervais.

Looking over his shoulder, her eyes took in the mansion.

"Yes. If that is what you wish."

"I can go to school here?" She hadn't even looked into programs around here, but she could. There were ways to make this work. Now that she knew, beyond a shadow of a doubt, that he loved her.

"Yes. If that is what you wish," he said again, those final words making it clear he understood her need for control over her life.

"We bring up our children here?"

"Yes, and in your country, too, whenever possible, if you wish. And most of all I hope that you'll do all of that as my wife." He squeezed her hand, brought her to a standing position.

Erika looked up at him, reading his eyes. "As simple as that?"

Pulling her into him, he shook his head. "Not simple at all. But very logical."

"Love as a logical emotion?" The idea tickled her.

"The love I feel for you defies any logic it's so incredible. It fills every corner of me. But I do know that my plan to work harder than I've ever worked at anything in my life to make you happy? Yes, that will be a plan I'm not leaving to chance. I will make that a conscious choice. But if you need time to decide—"

She cupped his face in her hands. "I do not need any more time at all. Yes."

"Yes?" Lines of excitement and relief tugged at his face.

She breathed in the scent of him, feeling balanced and renewed. Sure, for the first time in weeks, that this was where she was supposed to be.

"Yes, I love you and I will move in with you. I will go to school here. I will have our children here. And most of all, yes, I will marry you."

He gathered her closer, a sigh of relief racking his big, strong body. "Thank God."

"How did I ever get so lucky to meet and fall for such a wonderfully stubborn man?"

"We knew that day we met."

"In spite of logic."

"Instincts. With instincts like ours, we will make a winning team—" he rested his mouth on hers "—for life."

* * * * *

NEVER TOO LATE
Brenda Jackson

Chapter 1

Twelve days and counting…

Pushing a lock of twisted hair that had fallen in her face behind her ear, Sienna Bradford, soon to become Sienna Davis once again, straightened her shoulders as she walked into the cabin she'd once shared with her husband—soon-to-be ex-husband.

She glanced around. Had it been just three years ago when Dane had brought her here for the first time? Three years ago when the two of them had sat there in front of the fireplace after making love, and planned their wedding? Promising that no matter what, their marriage would last forever? She took a deep breath knowing that for them, forever would end in twelve days in Judge Ratcliff's chambers.

Just thinking about it made her heart ache, but she

decided it wouldn't help matters to have a pity party.
What was done was done and things just hadn't worked
out between her and Dane like they'd hoped. There was
nothing to do now but move on with her life. But first,
according to a letter her attorney had received from
Dane's attorney a few days ago, she had ten days to
clear out any and all of her belongings from the cabin,
and the sooner she got the task done, the better. Dane
had agreed to let her keep the condo if she returned full
ownership of the cabin to him. She'd had no problem
with that, since he had owned it before they married.

Sienna crossed the room, shaking off the March chill.
According to forecasters, a snowstorm was headed toward the Smoky Mountains within the next seventy-
two hours, which meant she had to hurry and pack up
her stuff and take the two-hour drive back to Charlotte.
Once she got home she intended to stay inside and curl
up in bed with a good book. Sienna smiled, thinking
that a "do nothing" weekend was just what she needed
in her too frantic life.

Her smile faded when she considered that since starting her own interior decorating business a year and a
half ago, she'd been extremely busy—and she had to
admit that was when her marital problems with Dane
had begun.

Sienna took a couple of steps toward the bedroom
to begin packing her belongings when she heard the
sound of the door opening. Turning quickly, she suddenly remembered she had forgotten to lock the door.
Not smart when she was alone in a secluded cabin high
up in the mountains, and a long way from civilization.

A scream quickly died in her throat when the person who walked in—standing a little over six feet with dark eyes, close-cropped black hair, chestnut coloring and a medium build—was none other than her soon-to-be ex.

From the glare on his face, she could tell he wasn't happy to see her. But so what? She wasn't happy to see him, either, and couldn't help wondering why he was there.

Before she could swallow the lump in her throat to ask, he crossed his arms over his broad chest, intensified his glare and said in that too sexy voice she knew so well, "I thought that was your car parked outside, Sienna. What are you doing here?"

Chapter 2

Dane wet his suddenly dry lips and immediately decided he needed a beer. Lucky for him there was a six-pack in the refrigerator from the last time he'd come to the cabin. But he didn't intend on moving an inch until Sienna told him what she was doing there.

She was nervous, he could tell. Well, that was too friggin bad. She was the one who'd filed for the divorce—he hadn't. But since she had made it clear that she wanted him out of her life, he had no problem giving her what she wanted, even if the pain was practically killing him. But she'd never know that.

"What do you think I'm doing here?" she asked smartly, reclaiming his absolute attention.

"If I knew, I wouldn't have asked," he said, giving her the same unblinking stare. And to think that at one time he actually thought she was his whole world. At some point during their marriage she had changed and transitioned into quite a character—someone he was certain he didn't know anymore.

She met his gaze for a long, level moment before placing her hands on her hips. Doing so drew his attention to her body; a body he'd seen naked countless times, a body he knew as well as his own; a body he used to ease into during the heat of passion to receive pleasure so keen and satisfying, just thinking about it made him hard.

"The reason I'm here, Dane Bradford, is because your attorney sent mine this nasty little letter demanding that I remove my stuff within ten days, and this weekend was better than next weekend. However, no thanks to you, I still had to close the shop early to beat traffic and the bad weather."

He actually smiled at the thought of her having to do that. "And I bet it almost killed you to close your shop early. Heaven forbid. You probably had to cancel a couple of appointments. Something I could never get you to do for me."

Sienna rolled her eyes. They'd had this same argument over and over again and it all boiled down to the same thing. He thought her job meant more to her than he did because of all the time she'd put into it. But what really irked her with that accusation was that before she'd even entertained the idea of quitting her job and embarking on her own business, they had talked about it and what it would mean. She would have to work her butt off and network to build a new clientele; and then there would be time spent working on decorating proposals, spending long hours in many beautiful homes of the rich and famous. And he had understood and had been supportive...at least in the beginning.

But then he began complaining that she was spending too much time away from home, away from him. Things only got worse from there, and now she was a woman who had gotten married at twenty-four and was getting divorced at twenty-seven.

"Look, Dane, it's too late to look back, reflect and complain. In twelve days you'll be free of me and I'll be free of you. I'm sure there's a woman out there who has the time and patience to—"

"Now, that's a word you don't know the meaning of, Sienna," Dane interrupted. "*Patience.* You were always in a rush, and your tolerance level for the least little thing was zero. Yeah, I know I probably annoyed the hell out of you at times. But then there were times you annoyed me, as well. Neither of us is perfect."

Sienna let out a deep breath. "I never said I was perfect, Dane."

"No, but you sure as hell acted like you thought you were, didn't you?"

Chapter 3

Dane's question struck a nerve. Considering her background, how could he assume Sienna thought she was perfect? She had come from a dysfunctional family if ever there was one. Her mother hadn't loved her father, her father loved all women except her mother, and neither seemed to love their only child. Sienna had always combated lack of love with doing the right thing, thinking that if she did, her parents would eventually love her. It didn't work. But still, she had gone through high school and college being the good girl, thinking being good would eventually pay off and earn her the love she'd always craved.

In her mind, it had when she'd met Dane, the man least likely to fall in love with her. He was the son of the millionaire Bradfords who'd made money in land development. She hadn't been his family's choice and they made sure she knew it every chance they got. Whenever she was around them, they made her feel inadequate, like she didn't measure up to their society friends, and since she didn't come from a family with a prestigious background, she wasn't good enough for their son.

She bet they wished they'd never hired the company she'd been working for to decorate their home. That's how she and Dane had met. She'd been going over fabric swatches with his mother and he'd walked in after playing a game of tennis. The rest was history. But the question of the hour was: Had she been so busy trying to succeed the past year and a half, trying to be the perfect business owner, that she eventually alienated the one person who'd mattered most to her?

"Can't answer that. Can you?" Dane said, breaking into her thoughts. "Maybe that will give you something to think about twelve days from now when you put your John Hancock on the divorce papers. Now if you'll excuse me, I have something to do," he said, walking around her toward the bedroom.

"Wait. You never said why *you're* here!"

He stopped. The intensity of his gaze sent shivers of heat through her entire body. And it didn't help matters that he was wearing jeans and a dark brown leather bomber jacket that made him look sexy as hell... as usual. "I was here a couple of weekends ago and left something behind. I came to get it."

"Were you alone?" The words rushed out before she could hold them back and immediately she wanted to smack herself. The last thing she wanted was for him to think she cared…even if she did.

He hooked his thumbs in his jeans and continued to hold her gaze. "Would it matter to you if I weren't?"

She couldn't look at him, certain he would see her lie when she replied, "No, it wouldn't matter. What you do is none of my business."

"That's what I thought." And then he walked off toward the bedroom and closed the door.

Sienna frowned. That was another thing she didn't like about Dane. He never stayed around to finish one of their arguments. Thanks to her parents she was a pro at it, but Dane would always walk away after giving some smart parting remark that only made her that much more angry. He didn't know how to fight fair. He didn't know how to fight at all. He'd come from a family too dignified for such nonsense.

Moving toward the kitchen to see if there was anything of hers in there, Sienna happened to glance out the window.

"Oh, my God," she said, rushing over to the window. It was snowing already. No, it wasn't just snowing… There was a full-scale blizzard going on outside. What happened to the seventy-two-hour warning?

She heard Dane when he came out of the bedroom. He looked beyond her and out the window, uttering one hell of a curse word before quickly walking to the door, slinging it open and stepping outside.

In just that short period of time, everything was beginning to turn white. The last time they'd had a sudden snowstorm such as this had been a few years ago. It had been so bad the media had nicknamed it the "Beast from the East."

It seemed the Beast was back and it had turned downright spiteful. Not only was it acting ugly outside, it had placed Sienna in one hell of a predicament. She was stranded in a cabin in the Smoky Mountains with her soon-to-be ex. Things couldn't get any more bizarre than that.

Chapter 4

Moments later, when Dane stepped back into the cabin, slamming the door behind him, Sienna could tell he was so mad he could barely breathe.

"What's wrong, Dane? You being forced to cancel a date tonight?" she asked snidely. A part of her was still upset at the thought that he might have brought someone here a couple of weekends ago when they weren't officially divorced yet. The mere fact they had been separated for six months didn't count. She hadn't gone out with anyone. Indulging in a relationship with another man hadn't even crossed her mind.

He took a step toward her and she refused to back up. She was determined to maintain her ground and her composure, although the intense look in his eyes was causing crazy things to happen to her body, like it normally did whenever they were alone for any period of time. There may have been a number of things wrong with their marriage, but lack of sexual chemistry had never been one of them.

"Do you know what this means?" he asked, his voice shaking in anger.

She tilted her head to one side. "Other than I'm being forced to remain here with you for a couple of hours, no, I don't know what it means."

She saw his hands ball into fists at his sides and knew he was probably fighting the urge to strangle her. "We're not talking about hours, Sienna. Try days. Haven't you been listening to the weather reports?"

She glared at him. "Haven't you? I'm not here by myself."

"Yes, but I thought I could come up here and in ten minutes max get what I came for, and leave before the bad weather kicked in."

Sienna regretted that she hadn't been listening to the weather reports, at least not in detail. She'd known that a snowstorm was headed toward the mountains within seventy-two hours, which was why she'd thought, like Dane, that she had time to rush and get in and out before the nasty weather hit. Anything other than that, she was clueless. And what was he saying about them being up here for days instead of hours? "Yes, I did listen to the weather reports, but evidently I missed something."

He shook his head. "Evidently you missed a lot, if you think this storm is going to blow over in a couple of hours. According to forecasters, what you see isn't the worst of it, and because of that unusual cold front hovering about in the east, it may last for days."

She swallowed deeply. The thought of spending *days* alone in a cabin with Dane didn't sit well with her. "How many days are we talking about?"

"Try three or four."

She didn't want to try any at all, and as she continued to gaze into his eyes she saw a look of worry replace the anger in their dark depths. Then she knew what had him upset.

"Do we have enough food and supplies up here to hold us for three or four days?" she asked, as she began to nervously gnaw on her lower lip. The magnitude of the situation they were in was slowly dawning on her, and when he didn't answer immediately she knew they were in trouble.

Chapter 5

Dane saw the panic that suddenly lined Sienna's face. He wished he could say he didn't give a damn, but there was no way that he could. This woman would always matter to him whether she was married to him or not. From the moment he had walked into his father's study that day and their gazes had connected, he had known then, as miraculous at it had seemed, and without a word spoken between them, that he was meant to love her. And for a while he had convinced her of that, but not anymore. Evidently, at some point during their marriage, she began believing otherwise.

"Dane?"

He rubbed his hand down his face, trying to get his thoughts together. Given the situation they were in, he knew honesty was foremost. But then he'd always been honest with her, however, he doubted she could say the same for herself. "To answer your question, Sienna, I'm not sure. Usually I keep the place well stocked of everything, but like I said earlier, I was here a couple of weekends ago, and I used a lot of the supplies then."

He refused to tell her that in a way it had been her fault. Receiving those divorce papers had driven him here, to wallow in self-pity, vent out his anger and drink his pain away with a bottle of Johnny Walker Red. "I guess we need to go check things out," he said, trying not to get as worried as she was beginning to look.

He followed her into the kitchen, trying not to watch the sway of her hips as she walked in front of him. The hot, familiar sight of her in a pair of jeans and pullover sweater had him cursing under his breath and summoning up a quick remedy for the situation he found himself in. The thought of being stranded for any amount of time with Sienna wasn't good.

He stopped walking when she flung open the refrigerator. His six-pack of beer was still there, but little else. But then he wasn't studying the contents of the refrigerator as much as he was studying her. She was bent over, looking inside, but all he could think of was another time he had walked into this kitchen and found her in that same position, and wearing nothing more than his T-shirt that had barely covered her bottom. It hadn't taken much for him to go into a crazed fit of lust and quickly remove his pajama bottoms and take her right then and there, against the refrigerator, giving them both the orgasm of a lifetime.

"Thank goodness there are some eggs in here," she

said, intruding on his heated thoughts down memory lane. "About half a dozen. And there's a loaf of bread that looks edible. There's some kind of meat in the freezer, but I'm not sure what it is, though. Looks like chicken."

She turned around and her pouty mouth tempted him to kiss it, devour it and make her moan. He watched her sigh deeply and then she gave him a not-so-hopeful gaze and said, "Our rations don't look good, Dane. What are we going to do?"

Chapter 6

Sienna's breath caught when the corners of Dane's mouth tilted in an irresistible smile. She'd seen the look before. She knew that smile and she also recognized that bulge pressing against his zipper. She frowned. "Don't even think it, Dane."

He leaned back against the kitchen counter. Hell, he wanted to do more than think it, he wanted to do it. But, of course, he would pretend he hadn't a clue as to what she was talking about. "What?"

Her frown deepened. "And don't act all innocent with me. I know what you were thinking."

A smile tugged deeper at Dane's lips knowing she probably did. There were some things a man couldn't hide and a rock-solid hard-on was one of them. He decided not to waste his time and hers pretending the chemistry between them was dead when they both knew it was still very much alive. "Don't ask me to apologize. It's not my fault you have so much sex appeal and my desire for you is automatic, even when we're headed for divorce court."

Dane saying the word *divorce* was a stark reminder that their life together, as they once knew it, would be over in twelve days. "Let's get back to important matters, Dane, like our survival. On a positive note, we might be able to make due if we cut back on meals, which may be hard for you with your ferocious appetite."

A wicked sounding chuckle poured from his throat. "Which one?"

Sienna swallowed as her pulse pounded in response to Dane's question. She was quickly reminded, although she wished there was some way she could forget, that her husband…or soon-to-be ex…did have two appetites. One was of a gastric nature and the other purely sexual. Thoughts of the purely sexual one had intense heat radiating all through her. Dane had devoured every inch of her body in ways she didn't even want to think about. Especially now.

She placed her hands on her hips knowing he was baiting her; really doing a hell of a lot more than that. He was stirring up feelings inside her that were making it hard for her to think straight. "Get serious, Dane."

"I am." He then came to stand in front of her. "Did you bring anything with you?"

She lifted a brow. "Anything like what?"

"Stuff to snack on. You're good for that. How you do it without gaining a pound is beyond me."

She shrugged, refusing to tell him that she used to work it off with all those in-bed, out-of-bed exercises they used to do. If he hadn't noticed then she wouldn't tell him that in six months without him in her bed, she had gained five pounds. "I might have a candy bar or two in the car."

He smiled. "That's all?"

She rolled her eyes upward. "Okay, okay, I might have a couple of bags of chips, too." She decided not to mention the three boxes of Girl Scout cookies that had been purchased that morning from a little girl standing in front of a grocery store.

"I hadn't planned to spend the night here, Dane. I had merely thought I could quickly pack things and leave."

He nodded. "Okay, I'll get the snacks from your car while I'm outside checking on some wood we'll need for the fire. The power is still on, but I can't see that lasting too much longer. I wished I would have gotten that generator fixed."

Her eyes widened in alarm. "You didn't?"

"No. So you might want to go around and gather up all the candles you can. And there should be a box of matches in one of these drawers."

"Okay."

Dane turned to leave. He then turned back around. She was nibbling on her bottom lip as he assumed she would be. "And stop worrying. We're going to make it."

When he walked out the room, Sienna leaned back against the closed refrigerator, thinking those were the exact words he'd said to her three years ago when he had asked her to marry him. Now she *was* worried because they didn't have a proved track record.

Chapter 7

After putting on the snow boots he kept at the cabin, Dane made his way out the doors, grateful for the time he wouldn't be in Sienna's presence. Being around her and still loving her like he did was hard. Even now he didn't know the reason for the divorce, other than what was noted in the papers he'd been served that day a few weeks ago. Irreconcilable differences...whatever the hell that was supposed to mean.

Sienna hadn't come to him so they could talk about any problems they were having. He had come home one day and she had moved out. He still was at a loss as to what could have been so wrong with their marriage that she could no longer see a future for them.

He would always recall that time as being the lowest point in his life. For days it was as if a part of him was missing. It had taken a while to finally pull himself together and realize she wasn't coming back no matter how many times he'd asked her to. And all it took was the receipt of that divorce petition to make him realize that Sienna wanted him out of her life, and actually believed that whatever issues kept them apart couldn't be resolved.

A little while later Dane had gathered more wood to put with the huge stack already on the back porch, glad that at least, if nothing else, they wouldn't freeze to death. The cabin was equipped with enough toiletries to hold them for at least a week, which was a good thing. And he hadn't wanted to break the news to Sienna that the meat in the freezer wasn't chicken, but deer meat that one of his clients had given him a couple of weeks ago after a hunting trip. It was good to eat, but he knew Sienna well enough to know she would have to be starving before she would consume any of it.

After rubbing his icy hands on his jeans, he stuck them into his pockets to keep them from freezing. Walking around the house, he strolled over to her car, opened the door and found the candy bars, chips and... Girl Scout cookies, he noted, lifting a brow. She hadn't mentioned them, and he saw they were her favorite kind, as well as his. He quickly recalled the first year they were married and how they shared the cookies as a midnight snack after making love. He couldn't help but smile as he remembered that night and others where they had spent time together, not just in bed but cooking in the kitchen, going to movies, concerts, parties, having picnics and just plain sitting around and talking for hours.

He suddenly realized that one of the things that had been missing from their marriage for a while was communication. When had they stopped talking? The first thought that grudgingly came to mind was when she'd begun bringing work home, letting it intrude on what had always been their time together. That's when they had begun living in separate worlds.

Dane breathed in deeply. He wanted to get back into Sienna's world and he definitely wanted her back in his. He didn't want a divorce. He wanted to keep his wife but he refused to resort to any type of manipulating, dominating or controlling tactics to do it. What he and Sienna needed was to use this weekend to keep it honest and talk openly about what had gone wrong with their marriage. They would go further by finding ways to resolve things. He still loved her and wanted to believe that deep down she still loved him.

There was only one way to find out.

Chapter 8

Sienna glanced around the room seeing all the lit candles and thinking just how romantic they made the cabin look. Taking a deep breath, she frowned in irritation, thinking that romance should be the last thing on her mind. Dane was her soon-to-be ex-husband. Whatever they once shared was over, done with, had come to a screeching end.

If only the memories weren't so strong...

She glanced out the window and saw him piling wood on the back porch. Never in her wildest dreams would she have thought her day would end up this way, with her and Dane being stranded together at the cabin—a place they always considered as their favorite getaway spot. During the first two years of their marriage, they would come here every chance they got, but in the past year she could recall them coming only once. Somewhere along the way she had stopped allowing them time even for this.

She sighed deeply, recalling how important it had been to her at the beginning of their marriage for them to make time to talk about matters of interest, whether trivial or important. They had always been attuned to each other, and Dane had always been a good listener, which to her conveyed a sign of caring and respect. But the last couple of times they had tried to talk ended up with them snapping at each other, which only built bitterness and resentment.

The lights blinked and she knew they were about to go out. She was glad that she had taken the initiative to go into the kitchen and scramble up some eggs earlier. And she was inwardly grateful that if she had to get stranded in the cabin during a snowstorm that Dane was here with her. Heaven knows she would have been a basket case had she found herself up here alone.

The lights blinked again before finally going out, but the candles provided the cabin with plenty of light. Not sure if the temperatures outside would cause the pipes to freeze, she had run plenty of water in the bathtub and kitchen sink, and filled every empty jug with water for them to drink. She'd also found batteries to put in the radio so they could keep up with any reports on the weather.

"I saw the lights go out. Are you okay?"

Sienna turned around. Dane was leaning in the doorway with his hands stuck in the pockets of his jeans. The pose made him look incredibly sexy. "Yes, I'm okay. I was able to get the candles all lit and there are plenty more."

"That's good."

"Just in case the pipes freeze and we can't use the shower, I filled the bathtub up with water so we can take a bath that way." At his raised brow she quickly added, "Separately, of course. And I made sure I filled plenty of bottles of drinking water, too."

He nodded. "Sounds like you've been busy."

"So have you. I saw through the window when you put all that wood on the porch. It will probably come in handy."

He moved away from the door. "Yes, and with the electricity out I need to go ahead and get the fire started."

Sienna swallowed as she watched him walk toward her on his way to the fireplace, and not for the first time she thought about how remarkably handsome he was. He had that certain charisma that made women get hot all over just looking at him.

It suddenly occurred to her that he'd already got a fire started, and the way it was spreading through her was about to make her burst into flames.

Chapter 9

"You okay?" Dane asked Sienna as he walked toward her with a smile.

She nodded and cleared her throat. "Yes, why do you ask?"

"Because you're looking at me funny."

"Oh." She was vaguely aware of him walking past her to kneel in front of the fireplace. She turned and watched him, saw him move the wood around before taking a match and lighting it to start a fire. He was so good at kindling things, whether wood or the human body.

"If you like, I can make something for dinner," she decided to say, otherwise she would continue to stand there and say nothing while staring at him. It was hard trying to be normal in a rather awkward situation.

"What are our options?" he asked without looking around.

She chuckled. "An egg sandwich and tea. I made both earlier before the power went off."

He turned at that and his gaze caught hers. A smile crinkled his eyes. "Do I have a choice?"

"Not if you want to eat."

"What about those Girl Scout cookies I found in your car?"

Her eyes narrowed. "They're off-limits. You can have one of the candy bars, but the cookies are mine."

His mouth broke into a wide grin. "You have enough cookies to share, so stop being selfish."

He turned back around and she made a face at him behind his back. He was back to stoking the fire and her gaze went to his hands. Those hands used to be the givers of so much pleasure and almost ran neck and neck with his mouth…but not quite. His mouth was in a class by itself. But still, she could recall those same hands, gentle, provoking, moving all over her body; touching her everywhere and doing things to her that mere hands weren't suppose to do. However, she never had any complaints.

"Did you have any plans for tonight, Sienna?"

His words intruded into her heated thoughts. "No, why?"

"Just wondering. You thought I had a date tonight. What about you?"

She shrugged. "No. As far as I'm concerned, until we sign those final papers, I'm still legally married and wouldn't feel right going out with someone."

He turned around and locked his eyes with hers. "I know what you mean," he said. "I wouldn't feel right going out with someone else."

Heat seeped through her every pore with his words. "So you haven't been dating, either?"

"No."

There were a number of questions she wanted to ask him—how he spent his days, his nights, what his family thought of their pending divorce, what he thought of it, was he ready for it to be over for them to go their separate ways—but there was no way she could ask him any of those things. "I guess I'll go put dinner on the table."

He chuckled. "An egg sandwich and tea?"

"Yes." She turned to leave.

"Sienna?"

She turned back around. "Yes?"

"I don't like being stranded, but since I am, I'm glad it's with you."

For a moment she couldn't say anything, then she cleared her throat while backing up a couple of steps. "Ah, yeah right, same here." She backed up some more then said, "I'll go set out the food now." And then she turned and quickly left the room.

Chapter 10

Sienna glanced up when she heard Dane walk into the kitchen and smiled. "Your feast awaits you."

"Whoopee."

She laughed. "Hey, I know the feeling. I'm glad I had a nice lunch today in celebration. I took on a new client."

Dane came and joined her at the table. "Congratulations."

"Thank you."

She took a bite of her scrambled egg sandwich and a sip of her tea and then said, "It's been a long time since you seemed genuinely pleased with my accomplishments."

He glanced up after taking a sip of his own tea and stared at her for a moment. "I know and I'm sorry about that. It was hard being replaced by your work, Sienna."

She lifted her head and stared at him, met his gaze. She saw the tightness of his jaw and the firm set of his mouth. He actually believed that something could replace him with her and knowing that hit a raw and sensitive nerve. "My work never replaced you, Dane. Why did you begin feeling that way?"

Dane leaned back in his chair, tilted his head slightly. He was more than mildly surprised with her question. It was then he realized that she really didn't know. Hadn't a clue. This was the opportunity that he wanted; what he was hoping they would have. Now was the time to put aside anger, bitterness, foolish pride and whatever else was working at destroying their marriage. Now was the time for complete honesty. "You started missing dinner. Not once but twice, sometimes three times a week. Eventually, you stopped making excuses and didn't show up."

What he'd said was the truth. "But I was working and taking on new clients," she defended. "You said you would understand."

"And I did for a while and up to a point. But there is such a thing as common courtesy and mutual respect, Sienna. In the end I felt like I'd been thrown by the wayside, that you didn't care anymore about us, our love or our marriage."

She narrowed her eyes. "And why didn't you say something?"

"When? I was usually asleep when you got home and when I got up in the morning you were too sleepy to discuss anything. I invited you to lunch several times, but you couldn't fit me into your schedule."

"I had appointments."

"Yes, and I always felt because of it that your clients were more important."

"Still, I wished you would have let me know how you felt," she said, after taking another sip of tea.

"I did, several times. But you weren't listening."

She sighed deeply. "We used to know how to communicate."

"Yes, at one time we did, didn't we?" Dane said quietly. "But I'm also to blame for the failure of our marriage, our lack of communication. And then there were the problems you were having with my parents. When it came to you, I never hesitated letting my parents know when they were out of line and that I wouldn't put up with their treatment of you. But then I felt that at some point you needed to start believing that what they thought didn't matter and stand up to them.

"I honestly thought I was doing the right thing when I decided to just stay out of it and give you the chance to deal with them, to finally put them in their place. Instead, you let them erode away at your security and confidence to the point where you felt you had to prove you were worthy of them…and of me. That's what drove you to be so successful, wasn't it, Sienna? Feeling the need to prove something is what working all those long hours was all about, wasn't it?"

Chapter 11

Sienna quickly got up from the table and walked to the window. It was turning dark but she could clearly see that things hadn't let up. It was still snowing outside, worse than an hour before. She tried to concentrate on what was beyond that window and not on the question Dane had asked her.

"Sienna?"

Moments later she turned back around to face Dane, knowing he was waiting on her response. "What do you want me to say, Dane? Trust me, you don't want to get me started since you've always known how your family felt about me."

His brow furrowed sharply as he moved from the table to join her at the window, coming to stand directly in front of her. "And you've known it didn't matter one damn iota. Why would you let it continue to matter to you?"

She shook her head, tempted to bare her soul but fighting not to. "But you don't understand how important it was for your family to accept me, to love me."

Dane stepped closer, looked into eyes that were fighting to keep tears at bay.

"Wasn't my love enough, Sienna? I'd told you countless time that you didn't marry my family, you married me. I'm not proud of the fact that my parents think too highly of themselves and our family name at times, but I've constantly told you it didn't matter. Why can't you believe me?"

When she didn't say anything, he sighed deeply. "You've been around people with money before. Do all of them act like my parents?"

She thought of her best friend's family. The Steeles. "No."

"Then what should that tell you? They're my parents. I know that they aren't close to being perfect, but I love them."

"And I never wanted to do anything to make you stop loving them."

He reached up and touched her chin. "And that's what this is about, isn't it? Why you filed for a divorce. You thought that you could."

Sienna angrily wiped at a tear she couldn't contain any longer. "I didn't ever want you to have to choose."

Dane's heart ached. Evidently she didn't know just how much he loved her. "There wouldn't have been a choice to make. You're my wife. I love you. I will always love you. When we married, we became one."

He leaned down and brushed a kiss on her cheek, then several. He wanted to devour her mouth, deepen the kiss and escalate it to a level he needed it to be, but he couldn't. He wouldn't. What they needed was to talk, to communicate to try and fix whatever was wrong with their marriage. He pulled back. It was hard when he heard her soft sigh, her heated moan.

He gave in briefly to temptation and tipped her chin up, and placed a kiss on her lips. "There's plenty of hot water still left in the tank," he said softly, stroking her chin. "Go ahead and take a shower before it gets completely dark, and then I'll take one."

He continued to stroke her chin when he added, "Then what I want is for us to do something we should have done months ago, Sienna. I want us to sit down and talk. And I mean to really talk. Regain that level of communication we once had. And what I need to know more than anything is whether my love will ever be just enough for you."

Chapter 12

You're my wife. I love you. I will always love you. When we married, we became one.

Dane's words flowed through Sienna's mind as she stepped into the shower, causing a warm, fuzzy, glowing feeling to seep through her pores. Hope flared within her although she didn't want it to. She hadn't wanted to end her marriage, but when things had begun to get worse between her and Dane, she'd finally decided to take her in-laws' suggestion and get out of their son's life.

Even after three years of seeing how happy she and Dane were together, they still couldn't look beyond her past. They saw her as a nobody, a person who had married their son for his money. She had offered to sign a prenuptial before the wedding and Dane had scoffed at the suggestion, refusing to even draw one up. But still, his parents had made it known each time they saw her just how much they resented the marriage.

And no matter how many times Dane had stood up to them and had put them in their place regarding her, it would only be a matter of time before they resorted to their old ways again, though never in the presence of their son. Maybe Dane was right, and all she'd had to do was tell his parents off once and for all and that would be the end of it, but she never could find the courage to do it.

And what was so hilarious with the entire situation was that she had basically become a workaholic to become successful in her own right so they could see her as their son's equal in every way; and in trying to impress them she had alienated Dane to the point that eventually he would have gotten fed up and asked her for a divorce if she hadn't done so first.

After spending time under the spray of water, she stepped out of the shower, intent on making sure there was enough hot water left for Dane. She tried to put out of her mind the last time she had taken a shower in this stall, and how Dane had joined her in it.

Toweling off, she was grateful she still had some of her belongings at the cabin to sleep in. The last thing she needed was to parade around Dane half naked. Then they would never get any talking done.

She slipped into a T-shirt and a pair of sweatpants she found in one of the drawers. Dane wanted to talk. How could they have honest communication without getting into a discussion about his parents again? She crossed her arms, trying to ignore the chill she was beginning to feel in the air. In order to stay warm they would probably both have to sleep in front of the fireplace tonight. She didn't want to think about what the possibility of doing something like that meant.

While her cell phone still had life, she decided to let her best friend, Vanessa Steele, know that she wouldn't be returning to Charlotte tonight. Dane was right. Not everyone with money acted like his parents. The Steeles, owners of a huge manufacturing company in Charlotte, were just as wealthy as the Bradfords. But they were as down-to-earth as people could get, which proved that not everyone with a lot of money were snobs.

"Hello?"

"Van, it's Sienna."

"Sienna, I was just thinking about you. Did you make it back before that snowstorm hit?"

"No, I'm in the mountains, stranded."

"What! Do you want me to send my cousins to rescue you?"

Sienna smiled. Vanessa was talking about her four single male cousins, Chance, Sebastian, Morgan and Donovan Steele. Sienna had to admit that besides being handsome as sin, they were dependable to a fault. And of all people, she, Vanessa and Vanessa's two younger sisters, Taylor and Cheyenne, should know more than anyone since they had been notorious for getting into trouble while growing up and the brothers four had always been there to bail them out.

"No, I don't need your cousins to come and rescue me."

"What about Dane? You know how I feel about you

divorcing him, Sienna. He's still legally your husband and I think I should let him know where you are and let him decide if he should—"

"Vanessa," Sienna interrupted. "You don't have to let Dane know anything. He's here, stranded with me."

Chapter 13

"How was your shower?" Dane asked Sienna when she returned to the living room a short while later.

"Great. Now it's your turn to indulge."

"Okay." Dane tried not to notice how the candlelight was flickering over Sienna's features, giving them an ethereal glow. He shoved his hands into the pockets of his jeans and for a long moment he stood there staring at her.

She lifted a brow. "What's wrong?"

"I was just thinking how incredibly beautiful you are."

Sienna breathed in deeply, trying to ignore the rush of sensations she felt from his words. "Thank you." Dane had always been a man who'd been free with his compliments. Being apart from him made her realize that was one of the things she missed, among many others.

"I'll be back in a little while," he said before leaving the room.

When he was gone, Sienna remembered the conversation she'd had with Vanessa earlier. Her best friend saw her and Dane being stranded together on the mountain as a twist of fate that Sienna should use to her advantage. Vanessa further thought that for once, Sienna should stand up to the elder Bradfords and not struggle to prove herself to them. Dane had accepted her as she was and now it was time for her to be satisfied and happy with that; after all, she wasn't married to his parents.

A part of Sienna knew that Vanessa was right, but she had been seeking love from others for so long that she hadn't been able to accept that Dane's love was all the love she needed. Before her shower he had asked if his love was enough and now she knew that it was. It was past time for her to acknowledge that fact and to let him know it.

Dane stepped out the shower and began toweling off. The bathroom carried Sienna's scent and the honeysuckle fragrance of the shower gel she enjoyed using.

Given their situation, he really should be worried what they would be faced with if the weather didn't let up in a couple of days with the little bit of food they had. But for now the thought of being stranded here with Sienna overrode all his concerns about that. In his heart, he truly believed they would manage to get through any given situation. Now he had the task of convincing her of that.

He glanced down at his left hand and studied his wedding band. Two weeks ago when he had come here for his pity party, he had taken it off in anger and thrown it in a drawer. It was only when he had returned to Charlotte that he realized he'd left it here in the cabin. At first he had shrugged it off as having no significant meaning since he would be a divorced man in a month's time anyway, but every day he'd felt that a part of him was missing.

In addition to reminding him of Sienna's absence from his life, to Dane, his ring signified their love and the vows that they had made, and a part of him refused to give that up. That's what had driven him back here this weekend—to reclaim the one element of his marriage that he refused to part with yet. Something he felt was rightfully his.

It seemed his ring wasn't the only thing that was rightfully his that he would get the chance to reclaim. More than anything, he wanted his wife back.

Chapter 14

Dane walked into the living room and stopped in his tracks. Sienna sat in front of the fireplace, cross-legged, with a tray of cookies and two glasses of wine. He knew where the cookies had come from, but where the heck had she gotten the wine?

She must have heard him because she glanced over his way and smiled. At that moment he thought she was even more breathtaking than a rose in winter. She licked her lips and immediately he thought she was even more tempting than any decadent dessert.

He cleared his throat. "Where did the wine come from?"

She licked her lips again and his body responded in an unquestionable way. He hoped the candlelight was hiding the physical effect she was having on him. "I found it in one of the kitchen cabinets. I think it's the bottle that was left when we came here to celebrate our first anniversary."

His thoughts immediately remembered that weekend. She had packed a selection of sexy lingerie and he had enjoyed removing each and every piece. She had also given him, among other things, a beautiful gold watch with the inscription engraved, *The Great Dane*. He, in turn, had given her a lover's bracelet, which was similar to a diamond tennis bracelet except that each letter of her name was etched in six of the stones.

He could still remember the single tear that had fallen from her eye when he had placed it on her wrist. That had been a special time for them, memories he would always cherish. That knowledge tightened the love that surrounded his heart. More than anything, he was determined that they settle things this weekend. He needed to make her see that he was hers and she was his. For always.

His lips creased into a smile. "I see you've decided to share the cookies, after all," he said, crossing the room to her.

She chuckled as he dropped down on the floor beside her. "Either that or run the risk of you getting up during the night and eating them all." The firelight danced through the twists on her head, highlighting the medium brown coiled strands with golden flecks. He absolutely loved the natural looking hairstyle on her.

He lifted a dark brow. "Eating them all? Three boxes?"

Her smile grew soft. "Hey, you've been known to overindulge a few times."

He paused as heated memories consumed him, reminding him of those times he had overindulged, especially when it came to making love to her. He recalled one weekend they had gone at it almost nonstop. If she hadn't been on the pill there was no doubt in his mind that that single weekend would have made him a daddy. A very proud one, at that.

She handed him a glass of wine. "May I propose a toast?"

His smile widened. "To what?"

"The return of the Beast from the East."

He switched his gaze from her to glance out the window. Even in the dark he could see the white flecks coming down in droves. He looked back at her and cocked a brow. "We have a reason to celebrate this bad weather?"

She stared at him for a long moment, then said quietly, "Yes. The Beast is the reason we're stranded here together, and even with our low rations of food, I can't think of any other place I'd rather be…than here alone with you."

Chapter 15

Dane stared at Sienna and the intensity of that gaze made her entire body tingle, her nerve endings steam. It was pretty much like the day they'd met, when he'd walked into his father's study. She had looked up, their gazes had connected and the seriousness in the dark irises that had locked with hers had changed her life forever. She had fallen in love with him then and there.

Dane didn't say anything for a long moment as he continued to look at her, and then he lifted his wineglass and said huskily, "To the Beast...who brought me Beauty."

His words were like a sensuous stroke down her spine, and the void feeling she'd had during the past few months was slowly fading away. After the toast was made and they had both taken sips of their wine,

Dane placed his glass aside and then relieved her of hers. He then slowly leaned forward and captured her mouth, tasting the wine, relishing her delectable flavor. How had she gone without this for six months? How had she survived? she wondered as his tongue devoured hers, battering deep in the heat of her mouth, licking and sucking as he wove his tongue in and out between teeth, gum and whatever wanted to serve as a barrier.

He suddenly pulled back and stared at her. A smile touched the corners of his lips. "I could keep going and going, but before we go any further we need to talk, determine what brought us to this point so it won't ever be allowed to happen again. I don't want us to ever let anything or anyone have power, more control over the vows we made three years ago."

Sienna nodded, thinking the way the firelight was dancing over his dark skin was sending an erotic frisson up her spine. "All right."

He stood. "I'll be right back."

Sienna lifted a brow, wondering where he was going and watched as he crossed the room to open the desk drawer. Like her, he had changed into a T-shirt and a pair of sweats, and as she watched him she found it difficult to breathe. He moved in such a manly way, each movement a display of fine muscles and limbs and how they worked together in graceful coordination, perfect precision. Watching him only knocked her hormones out of whack.

He returned moments later with pens and paper in hand. There was a serious expression on his face when he handed her a sheet of paper and a pen and kept the same for himself. "I want us to write down all the things we feel went wrong with our marriage, being honest to include everything. And then we'll discuss them."

She looked down at the pen and paper and then back at him. "You want me to write them down?"

"Yes, and I'll do the same."

Sienna nodded and watched as he began writing on his paper, wondering what he was jotting down. She leaned back and sighed, wondering if she could air their dirty laundry on paper, but it seemed he had no such qualms. Most couples sought the helpful guidance of marriage counselors when they found themselves in similar situations, but she hadn't given them that chance. But at this point, she would do anything to save her marriage.

So she began writing, being honest with herself and with him.

Chapter 16

Dane finished writing and glanced over at Sienna. She was still at it and had a serious expression on her features. He studied the contours of her face and his gaze dropped to her neck, and he noticed the thin gold chain. She was still wearing the heart pendant he'd given her as a wedding gift.

Deep down, Dane believed this little assignment was what they needed as the first step in repairing what had gone wrong in their marriage. Having things written down would make it easier to stay focused and not go off on a tangent. And it made one less likely to give in to the power of the mind, the wills and emotions. He wanted them to concentrate on those destructive elements and forces that had eroded away at what should have been a strong relationship.

She glanced up and met his gaze as she put the pen aside. She gave him a wry smile. "Okay, that's it."

He reached out and took her hand in his, tightening his hold on it when he saw a look of uncertainty on her face. "All right, what do you have?"

She gave him a sheepish grimace. "How about you going first?"

He gently squeezed her hand. "How about if we go together? I'll start off and then we'll alternate."

She nodded. "What if we have the same ones?"

"That will be okay. We'll talk about all of them." He picked up his piece of paper.

"First on my list is communication."

Sienna smiled ruefully. "It's first on mine, too. And I agree that we need to talk more, without arguing, not that you argued. I think you would hold stuff in when I made you upset instead of getting it out and speaking your mind."

Dane stared at her for a moment, then a smile touched his lips. "You're right, you know. I always had to plug in the last word and I did it because I knew it would piss you off."

"Well, stop doing it."

He grinned. "Okay. The next time I'll hang around for us to talk through things. But then you're going to have to make sure that you're available when we need to talk. You can't let anything, not even your job, get in the way of us communicating."

"Okay, I agree."

"Now, what's next on your list?" he asked.

She looked up at him and smiled. "Patience. I know

you said that I don't have patience, but neither do you. But you used to."

Dane shook his head. "Yeah, I lost my patience when you did. I thought to myself, why should I be patient with you when you weren't doing the same with me? Sometimes I think you thought I enjoyed knowing you had a bad day or didn't make a sale, and that wasn't it at all. At some point what was suddenly important to you wasn't important to me anymore."

"And because of it, we both became detached," Sienna said softly.

"Yes, we did." He reached out and lifted her chin. "I promise to do a better job of being patient, Sienna."

"So will I, Dane."

They alternated, going down the list. They had a number of the same things on both lists and they discussed everything in detail, acknowledging their faults and what they could have done to make things better. They also discussed what they would do in the future to strengthen their marriage.

"That's all I have on my list," Dane said a while later. "Do you have anything else?"

Sienna's finger glided over her list. For a short while she thought about pretending she didn't have anything else, but they had agreed to be completely honest. They had definitely done so when they had discussed her spending more time at work than at home.

"So what's the last thing on your list, Sienna? What do you see as one of the things that went wrong with our marriage?"

She lifted her chin and met his gaze and said, "My inability to stand up to your parents."

He looked at her with deep, dark eyes. "Okay, then. Let's talk about that."

Chapter 17

Dane waited patiently for Sienna to begin talking and gently rubbed the backside of her hand while doing so. He'd known the issue of his parents had always been a challenge to her. Over the years, he had tried to make her see that how the elder Bradfords felt didn't matter. What he failed to realize, accept and understand was that it *did* matter...to her.

She had grown up in a family without love for so long that when they married, she not only sought his love, but that of his family. Being accepted meant a lot to her, and her expectations of the Bradfords, given how they operated and their family history, were too high.

They weren't a close-knit bunch, never had been and never would be. His parents had allowed their own parents to decide their future, including who they married.

When they had come of age, arranged marriages were the norm within the Bradfords' circle. His father had once confided to him one night after indulging in too many drinks that his mother had not been his choice for a wife. That hadn't surprised Dane, nor had it bothered him, since he would bet that his father probably hadn't been his mother's choice of a husband, either.

"I don't want to rehash the past, Dane," Sienna finally said softly, looking at the blaze in the fireplace instead of at him. "But something you said earlier tonight has made me think about a lot of things. You love your parents, but you've never hesitated in letting them know when you felt they were wrong, nor have you put up with their crap when it came to me."

She switched her gaze from the fire to him. "The problem is that *I* put up with their crap when it came to me. And you were right. I thought I had to actually prove something to them, show them I was worthy of you and your love. And I've spent the better part of a year and a half doing that and all it did was bring me closer and closer to losing you. I'm sure they've been walking around with big smiles on their faces since you got the divorce petition. But I refuse to let them be happy at my expense and my own heartbreak."

She scooted closer to Dane and splayed her hands against his chest. "It's time I became more assertive with your parents, Dane. Because it's not about them—it's about us. I refuse to let them make me feel unworthy any longer, because I am worthy to be loved by you. I don't have anything to prove. They either accept me as I am or not at all. The only person who matters anymore is you."

With his gaze holding hers, Dane lifted one of her hands off his chest and brought it to his lips, and placed a kiss on the palm. "I'm glad you've finally come to realize that, Sienna. And I wholeheartedly understand and agree. I was made to love you, and if my parents never accept that then it's their loss, not ours."

Tears constricted Sienna's throat and she swallowed deeply before she could find her voice to say, "I love you, Dane. I don't want the divorce. I never did. I want to belong to you and I want you to belong to me. I just want to make you happy."

"And I love you, too, Sienna, and I don't want the divorce, either. My life will be nothing without you being a part of it. I love you so much and I've missed you."

And with his heart pounding hard in his chest, he leaned over and captured her lips, intent on showing her just what he meant.

Chapter 18

This is homecoming, Sienna thought as she was quickly consumed by the hungry onslaught of Dane's kiss. All the hurt and anger she'd felt for six months was being replaced by passion of the most heated kind. All she could think about was the desire she was feeling being back in the arms of the man she loved and who loved her.

This was the type of communication she'd always loved, where she could share her thoughts, feelings and desires with Dane without uttering a single word. It was where their deepest emotions and what was in their inner hearts spoke for them, expressing things so eloquently and not leaving any room for misunderstandings.

He pulled back slightly, his lips hovering within inches of hers. He reached out and caressed her cheek, and as if she needed his taste again, her lips automatically parted. A slow, sensual acknowledgement of understanding tilted the corners of his mouth into a smile. Then he leaned closer and kissed her again, longer and harder, and the only thing she could do was to wrap her arms around him and silently thank God for reuniting her with this very special man.

Dane was hungry for the taste of his wife and at that moment, as his heart continued to pound relentlessly in his chest, he knew he had to make love to her, to show her in every way what she meant to him, had always meant to him and would always mean to him.

He pulled back slightly and the moisture that was left on her lips made his stomach clench. He leaned forward and licked them dry, or tried to, but her scent was driving him to do more. "Please let me make love to you, Sienna," he whispered, leaning down and resting his forehead against hers.

She leaned back and cupped his chin with her hand. "Oh, yes. I want you to make love to me, Dane. I've missed being with you so much I ache."

"Oh, baby, I love you." He pulled her closer, murmured the words in her twisted locks, kissed her cheek, her temple, her lips, and he cupped her buttocks, practically lifting her off the floor in the process. His breath came out harsh, ragged, as the chemistry between them sizzled. There was only one way to drench their fire.

He stretched out with her in front of the fireplace as he began removing her clothes and then his. Moments later, the blaze from the fire was a flickering light across their naked skin. And then he began kissing her all over, leaving no part of her untouched, determined to quench his hunger and his desire. He had missed the taste of her and was determined to be reacquainted in every way he could think of.

"Dane…"

Her tortured moan ignited the passion within him and he leaned forward to position his body over hers, letting his throbbing erection come to rest between her thighs, gently touching the entrance of her moist heat. He lifted his head to look down at her, wanting to see her expression the exact moment their bodies joined again.

Chapter 19

Sienna stared into Dane's eyes, the heat and passion she saw in them making her shiver. The love she recognized made her heart pound, and the desire she felt for him sent surges and surges of sensations through every part of her body, especially the area between her legs, making her thighs quiver.

"You're my everything, Sienna," he whispered as he began easing inside of her. His gaze was locked with hers as his voice came out in a husky tone. "I need you like I need air to breathe, water for thirst and food for nourishment. Oh, baby, my life has been so empty since you've been gone. I love and need you."

His words touched her and when he was embedded inside of her to the hilt, she arched her back, needing and wanting even more of him. She gripped his shoulders with her fingers as liquid fire seemed to flow to all parts of her body.

And at that moment she forgot everything—the Beast from the East, their limited supply of food and the fact they were stranded together in a cabin with barely enough heat. The only thing that registered in her mind was that they were together and expressing their love in a way that literally touched her soul.

He continued to stroke her, in and out, and with each powerful thrust into her body she moaned out his name and told him of her love. She was like a bow whose strings were being stretched to the limit each and every time he drove into her, and she met his thrusts with her own eager ones.

And then she felt it, the strength like a volcano erupting as he continued to stroke her to oblivion. Her body splintered into a thousand pieces as an orgasm ripped through her, almost snatching her breath away. And when she felt him buck, tighten his hold on her hips and thrust into her deeper, she knew that same powerful sensation had taken hold of him, as well.

"Sienna!"

He screamed her name and growled a couple of words that were incoherent to her ears. She tightened her arms around his neck, needing to be as close to him as she could get. She knew in her heart at that moment that things were going to be fine. She and Dane had proved that when it came to the power of love, it was never too late.

Sienna awoke the following morning naked, in front of the fireplace and cuddled in her husband's arms with a blanket covering them. After yawning, she raised her chin and glanced over at him and met his gaze head-on. The intensity in the dark eyes staring back at her shot heat through all parts of her body. She couldn't help but recall last night and how they had tried making up for all the time they had been apart.

"It's gone," Dane said softly, pulling her closer into his arms.

She lifted a brow. "What's gone?"

"The Beast."

She tilted her head to glance out the window and he was right. Although snow was still falling, it wasn't the violent blizzard that had been unleashed the day before. It was as if the weather had served the purpose it had come for and had made its exit. She smiled. Evidently, someone up there knew she and Dane's relationship was meant to be saved and had stepped in to salvage it.

She was about to say something when suddenly there was a loud pounding at the door. She and Dane looked at each other, wondering who would be paying them a visit to the cabin at this hour and in this weather.

Chapter 20

Sienna, like Dane, had quickly gotten dressed and was now staring at the four men who were standing in the doorway…those handsome Steele brothers. She smiled, shaking her head. Vanessa had evidently called her cousins to come rescue her, anyway.

"Vanessa called us," Chance Steele, the oldest of the pack, said by way of explanation. "It just so happened that we were only a couple of miles down the road at our own cabin." A smile touched his lips. "She was concerned that the two of you were here starving to death and asked us to share some of our rations."

"Thanks, guys," Dane said, gladly accepting the box Sebastian Steele was handing him. "Come on in. And although we've had plenty of heat to keep us warm, I have to admit our food supply was kind of low."

As soon as the four entered, all eyes went to Sienna. Although the brothers knew Dane because their families sometimes ran in the same social circles, as well as the fact that Dane and Donovan Steele had graduated from high school the same year, she knew their main concern was for her. She had been their cousin Vanessa's best friend for years, and as a result they had sort of adopted her as their little cousin, as well.

"You okay?" Morgan Steele asked her, although Sienna knew she had to look fine; probably like a woman who'd been made love to all night, and she wasn't ashamed of that fact. After all, Dane *was* her husband. But the Steeles knew about her pending divorce, so she decided to end their worries.

She smiled and moved closer to Dane. He automatically wrapped his arms around her shoulders and brought her closer to his side. "Yes, I'm wonderful," she said, breaking the subtle tension she felt in the room. "Dane and I have decided we don't want a divorce and intend to stay together and make our marriage work."

The relieved smiles on the faces of the four men were priceless. "That's wonderful. We're happy for you," Donovan Steele said, grinning.

"We apologize if we interrupted anything, but you know Vanessa," Chance said, smiling. "She wouldn't let up. We would have come sooner but the bad weather kept us away."

"Your timing was perfect," Dane said, grinning. "We appreciate you even coming out now. I'm sure the roads weren't their best."

"No, but my new truck managed just fine," Sebastian

said proudly. "Besides, we're going fishing later. We would invite you to join us, Dane, but I'm sure you can think of other ways you'd prefer to spend your time."

Dane smiled as he glanced down and met Sienna's gaze. "Oh, yeah, I can definitely think of a few."

The power had been restored and a couple of hours later, after eating a hefty breakfast of pancakes, sausage, grits and eggs, and drinking what Dane had to admit was the best coffee he'd had in a long time, Dane and Sienna were wrapped in each other's arms in the king-size bed. Sensations flowed through her just thinking about how they had ached and hungered for each other, and the fierceness of their lovemaking to fulfill that need and greed.

"Now will you tell me what brought you to the cabin?" Sienna asked, turning in Dane's arms and meeting his gaze.

"My wedding band." He then told her why he'd come to the cabin two weeks ago and how he'd left the ring behind. "It was as if without that ring on my finger, my connection to you was gone. I had to have it back so I came here for it."

Sienna nodded, understanding completely. That was one of the reasons she hadn't removed hers. Reaching out she cupped his stubble jaw in her hand and then leaned over and kissed him softly. "Together forever, Mr. Bradford."

Dane smiled. "Yes, Mrs. Bradford, together forever. We've proved that when it comes to true love, it's never too late."

* * * * *

REQUEST YOUR FREE BOOKS!
2 FREE NOVELS PLUS 2 FREE GIFTS!

⊕HARLEQUIN®

Desire

ALWAYS POWERFUL, PASSIONATE AND PROVOCATIVE

YES! Please send me 2 FREE Harlequin® Desire novels and my 2 FREE gifts (gifts are worth about $10). After receiving them, if I don't wish to receive any more books, I can return the shipping statement marked "cancel." If I don't cancel, I will receive 6 brand-new novels every month and be billed just $4.55 per book in the U.S. or $5.24 per book in Canada. That's a savings of at least 13% off the cover price! It's quite a bargain! Shipping and handling is just 50¢ per book in the U.S. and 75¢ per book in Canada.* I understand that accepting the 2 free books and gifts places me under no obligation to buy anything. I can always return a shipment and cancel at any time. Even if I never buy another book, the two free books and gifts are mine to keep forever.

225/326 HDN GH2P

Name	(PLEASE PRINT)

Address	Apt. #

City	State/Prov.	Zip/Postal Code

Signature (if under 18, a parent or guardian must sign)

Mail to the **Reader Service**:
IN U.S.A.: P.O. Box 1867, Buffalo, NY 14240-1867
IN CANADA: P.O. Box 609, Fort Erie, Ontario L2A 5X3

Want to try two free books from another line?
Call 1-800-873-8635 or visit www.ReaderService.com.

* Terms and prices subject to change without notice. Prices do not include applicable taxes. Sales tax applicable in N.Y. Canadian residents will be charged applicable taxes. Offer not valid in Quebec. This offer is limited to one order per household. Not valid for current subscribers to Harlequin Desire books. All orders subject to credit approval. Credit or debit balances in a customer's account(s) may be offset by any other outstanding balance owed by or to the customer. Please allow 4 to 6 weeks for delivery. Offer available while quantities last.

Your Privacy—The Reader Service is committed to protecting your privacy. Our Privacy Policy is available online at www.ReaderService.com or upon request from the Reader Service.

We make a portion of our mailing list available to reputable third parties that offer products we believe may interest you. If you prefer that we not exchange your name with third parties, or if you wish to clarify or modify your communication preferences, please visit us at www.ReaderService.com/consumerschoice or write to us at Reader Service Preference Service, P.O. Box 9062, Buffalo, NY 14240-9062. Include your complete name and address.

HD15

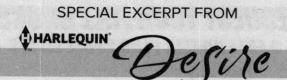
Claire looked completely panicked by the thought of Luca having access to her child.

Their child.

It seemed so wrong for him to have a child with a woman he'd never met. But now that he had a living, breathing daughter, he wasn't about to sit back and pretend it didn't happen. Eva was probably the only child he would ever have, and he'd already missed months of her life. That would not continue.

"We can and we will." Luca spoke up at last. "Eva is my daughter, and I've got the paternity test results to prove it. There's not a judge in the county of New York who won't grant me emergency visitation while we await our court date. They will say when and where and how often you have to give her to me."

Claire sat, her mouth agape at his words. "She's just a baby. She's only six months old. Why fight me for her just so you can hand her over to a nanny?"

Luca laughed at her presumptuous tone. "What makes you so certain I'll have a nanny for her?"

"You're a rich, powerful, unmarried businessman. You're better suited to run a corporation than to change a diaper. I'm willing to bet you don't have the first clue of how to care for an infant, much less the time."

Luca just shook his head and sat forward in his seat. "You know very little about me, *tesorino*, you've said so yourself, so don't presume anything about me."

Claire narrowed her gaze at him. She definitely didn't like him pushing her. And he was pushing her. Partially because he liked to see the fire in her eyes and the flush of her skin, and partially because it was necessary to get through to her.

Neither of them had asked for this to happen to them, but she needed to learn she wasn't in charge. They had to cooperate if this awkward situation was going to improve. He'd started off nice, politely requesting to see Eva, and he'd been flatly ignored. As each request was met with silence, he'd escalated the pressure. That's how they'd ended up here today. If she pushed him any further, he would start playing hardball. He didn't want to, but he would crush her like his restaurants' competitors.

"We can work together and play nice, or my lawyer here can make things very difficult for you. As he said, it's your choice."

"What are you suggesting, Mr. Moretti?" her lawyer asked.

"I'm suggesting we both take a little time away from our jobs and spend it together."

Don't miss
THE CEO'S UNEXPECTED CHILD
by Andrea Laurence, available March 2016 wherever
Harlequin® Desire books and ebooks are sold.

www.Harlequin.com

HDEXP0216